SHADOW NIGHTS

ARC I: INTO THE SHADOWS

Seishin

MILTON & HUGO L.L.C.
4407 Park Ave., Suite 5
Union City, NJ 07087, USA

Website: *www. miltonandhugo.com*
Hotline: *1- 888-778-0033*
Email: *info@miltonandhugo.com*

Ordering Information:
Quantity sales. Special discounts are granted to corporations, associations, and other organizations. For more information on these discounts, please reach out to the publisher using the contact information provided above.

Library of Congress Control Number: 2025919072
ISBN-13:   979-8-89285-650-8   [Paperback Edition]
                   979-8-89285-649-2   [Digital Edition]

Rev. date: 08/18/2025

CONTENTS

ACKNOWLEDGMENT

This story that you are about to read was made thanks to the support of many people.

I have to thank my friend from high school who motivated me to start writing in the first place and to continue writing this book throughout college. She was the first avid reader of my work, and for that, I'd give her everything. I loved the days when she would nag on me about every twist and turn my story, especially when, for a time, she gave me the evil eye for hurting her favorite character, Rex.

I have to thank my friend that helped guide my story through all the hurdles of the revision and editing process. Without her, I would've forever been lost in my work, never truly being able to know exactly where to move next in my story and, most importantly, in life. While I started writing the book at the end of my high school with high spirits, I finished it at a time when I was at my worst. Having her in my life really brought back my spirits and helped me focus on bettering myself.

I have to thank my family, that even when it seemed like they didn't, they wanted me to succeed from the moment I told them. They would harp on me to perfect small portions of what I had and to always cut the story in half. I didn't quite understand why, but it was their way of worrying about my health, and looking back now, I'm thankful for it. The best thing that happened, however, was when my brother stole my edited manuscript and brought it to school and came back telling me that I needed to give him a cleaner copy to read while at school. It was an exhilarating feeling, to say the least.

And finally, I have to thank you, the reader. I haven't met you personally, but from the bottom of my heart, thank you. You took a chance, spared a bit of your time, and finished the story I wanted to tell. Not many people would willingly do that, but you did. I couldn't ask anything more from you other than to continue to show that same love to the people around you. You are a hero, in my eyes, at least. I can't say this in words enough. Thank you so much for exploring my world.

PROLOGUE

The strong scent of alcohol and whisky flooded the room. As the sun slowly started to set over the horizon, the cool air of the night only made the bar atmosphere more appealing to those seeking a small release. Men and women of varying ages sat around tables, drinking all their troubles away, even just to escape them for the moment. All of them, save a single woman dressed in all black. She held a single bottle of whisky, untouched and filled to the brim, and was staring the bottle down with a motionless expression. She replaced the bottle down in front of her as she continued to loom over the beverage, completely ignoring the man that was sitting right next to her.

MAN: To think I'd find you here of all places.

He crossed his arm as he placed them on the counter, tilting his seat to face the woman. He, too, was dressed in a similar black as the woman. The woman barely took her eyes off the bottle as she weakly spoke out in a painful voice.

WOMAN: This was her favorite place in this whole rotten ass city. We'd come here every few weeks and suffer through it together. Now I have to bear it all for the both of us.

MAN: I know, she would tell me all abou—

The woman slammed the bottle over the man's hand as her tired voice slowly began to rise higher.

WOMAN: Shut. Up. You don't get to speak, not after what she did for you.

The man rubbed the back of his hand as he let out a hard sigh. Neither spoke for a while. Then the woman spoke again.

WOMAN: How are they taking it?

MAN: She's fine. We're all fine. Everyone but you. I've spent the past week *trying so fucking hard* to keep what's left of this cursed family sane, and—

WOMAN: She died so you could finally be a good father.

The man quickly choked on his own words, and the woman finally turned in her seat to face the man for the first time since the night started.

WOMAN: I don't care what those other freaks of yours say. You should've died in her place.

MAN: Then let me *fucking* fix this. I'm trying to *fix this!* What do I have to do for you to just come fucking home? Look at yourself. *You're a mess!*

WOMAN: And you have it better? How many times have I—

MAN: Don't even start bringing her into this. If you really cared, I wouldn't have to grab you from here.

The woman stood up from her chair and pulled the man closer to her.

WOMAN: (*Whispering into the man's ear*) Then do me one favor in your worthless life. Either die or give me her back. One or the other.

MAN: Fuck you. She's my daughter, not yours. She never was, and she never will.

In an instant, the woman smashed the bottle over the man's head as everyone in the bar turned to watch the scene play out. The man pulled himself off the floor, then he felt something wrap around his leg.

WOMAN: You are *nothing*! *All of you are nothing*! One day, you'll all be used as fuel for something much grander than I. *You'll see. You'll all see!*

The slowly growing crowd looked at that man as he signaled that she was just drunk. The signal made most of the crowd start to disperse. As fast as she had smashed the bottle over him, the woman looked down at the man as he struggled to pull himself up off the floor. The more he struggled, the tighter the grip on his leg got. It all came to a breaking point until the woman took an exhausted tone and the force was let go of the man. As it did, he noticed a small vine move away from his leg and closer to the woman before she started to leave. As she reached the door's edge, she looked back at the man with a dark smile.

WOMAN: Enjoy your last few moments with that girl. Sooner or later, she'll be mine.

She left as swiftly as the man found her. The man quickly got back to his feet to try and find her, but to no avail. He rubbed his head, to see a small trail of blood fall from his fingers onto the street outside.

MAN: *Fucking bitch.* Fine. At the very least, I know she's alive. *But what was that vine shit?* Whatever. Too tired for this shit. Way too late to stay out here any longer anyway.

CHAPTER

1

Present day

NEWS REPORTER: This just in, the recent case of kidnappings is still at an all-time high as the crime rate for the uptown and downtown area reaches an all-time high. The police force is run thin, with most of the force being worn out beyond belief. Here's what they have to say on the matter.

COP A: Yeah, sometimes I wish we had an extra hand in dealing with all of this.

NEWS REPORTER: With that, I'm Casy James, signing off the morning news.

The TV changed to a different channel to show several people standing outside of a TV store watching the news turn off for the morning, to the dismay of a few.

PERSON A: Man, this all sucks. Nothing in this shit city is getting better. Fuck.

PERSON B: All we can do now is pray for a miracle.

Several people started to walk away, leaving one young man to stare at his reflection in the window, taking all the noise into heart.

YOUNG MAN: A miracle. Maybe—

His thought was cut short at the shouts of a smaller boy from further down the street from him.

YOUNG BOY: Gavin! *If we don't hurry, we'll be late!*

GAVIN: *Sorry, Rex. I'm coming!*

The young man ran up to the other, and they both started to walk down the bustling city streets, avoiding any alleys and the everyday homeless person—all in attempt to get to both their schools on time. To the two of them, this was normal. Well, normal for one of them. As they both reached an elementary school, the younger of them gave a wave as he walked inside.

GAVIN: Later, Rex. See you at the house later.

REX: Later. I already called dibs on the TV back home.

With that, the two brothers parted ways, leaving Gavin alone to walk himself to school.

—◆—

Now as fun as it has been narration for you, dear reader, this isn't my story to tell, and it's best if you see the world from his point of view. Speaking of, he should probably hurry and get to class.

—◆—

GAVIN: Yeah, right. He always has dibs on it. All right, let
　　　see what I have to deal with today.

I made my way down an alley, avoiding people that wanted to ask me questions. This already was starting to be a long day. It didn't take me long to get to my school. I walked into the crowded hallways and kids walking up and down the halls. I just ignored most of it all and got to my class and sat in a chair. It was still extremely early in the morning as I looked out the window next to my seat. Usually, I'd use this time to finish any extra homework I had piled up, but today I just laid my head down on the table and drifted off to sleep. I had a lot on my mind

2

from the last few days. Maybe a nap can help clear my mind and put it all in a better light.

Two days ago

The sudden halt from train wheels woke me up from my aimless drifting. I really need to get a better sleep schedule soon. Several late nights of just staring at books isn't healthy for anyone. The train doors opened on its last stop, and I grabbed a bag of groceries that was next to me. I hopped out of my seat with a long yawn, and I walked out to the empty suburban city side. It's really nice out here, with barely anyone around for miles. It does suck every now and then when I have to make food runs for my mom, but seeing the amount of pure nature always fills me with enough joy to make up for it. The sun was starting to set as I walked down a very familiar path, humming a small tune to myself. This should've been an easy task, but call it fate or a case of bad luck, I was going to take a long detour home.

GAVIN: And the burn season drift, hmm, hmm, hmm, and they hold the keys that break beyond your *faaaaaaaaith*...

I wasn't looking where I was going and accidentally stepped on the tail of this white cat. Its loud screech of pain snapped me out of my mini jam out, causing me to drop a few packets of tuna out of my bag.

GAVIN: Oops, sorry about that, little guy. Didn't see ya there.

The cat started to eye at the tuna, then back at me as I was getting back to my senses. I could see in its eyes what it was about to do.

GAVIN: Hey! Don't you even—

The cat instantly grabbed the tuna and started to make its escape. I quickly got back up to my feet and started the chase with the cat into several bushes, hopping in and out of them, constantly getting stuck at times. After a long chase, I went for a dive, knocking the tuna packets out from its mouth.

GAVIN: *Ha!* Got ya, and I'll be taking *that*! Now get out of here.

The cat looked a bit angry at me before looking around us. It was then that I also looked around a bit with the cat. The area we once looked at was completely foreign to me. Where did we both run off to? It was some strange area that was covered in dark dead-looking trees. The sky had turned pitch black with no stars anywhere. I would've said it wasn't night if the moon didn't look a strange color of red, like a blood moon. It almost looked like a giant rose in the sky, weirdly enough.

GAVIN: Where the—no, no, just focus and calm down.
    Need to get home.

I decided to try and retrace my steps, which led to just getting lost more. It had been what felt like fifteen minutes when I eventually sat down on a dark tree stump with the cat following right beside me, lying at my feet, looking at me with what I could only describe as boredom.

GAVIN: So you don't know how to get out here either. Shit.

I sat there for a second before a strange light caught my attention deep within the trees. I stared at it, bewildered for a second as the wind seemed like it was talking to me.

"S…a…v…e…h…i…m…," it said to me.

I started to look around, to not make sure I was crazy. When I stood up, the wind started to push me toward the light. The wind voice got louder as I was pushed deeper into the light. The cat ran off somewhere, leaving me to get pushed into an open area and fell over myself. When I finally got back to my feet, I only saw one thing in front of me: a strange dark light that felt strangely comforting. I reached out to it and…

Present day

TEACHER: *Gavin!*

GAVIN: *I'm up. I'm up!*

The forces of a ruler slap had woken me up from my small nap as students around me started to laugh at my sudden awakening. The teacher then pointed to a hard equation on the board a few times.

TEACHER: Well then, if you want to start slacking so much
    then, let's see if you can answer this question.

4

I let out a low yawn, and I heard small murmurs from my classmates.

STUDENT A: Heh, dumbass. Hey, Kim. Look.

STUDENT B: What a weirdo. Loser face too.

STUDENT C: Man, I really should've eaten before class. Maybe I'll ask Jeff for some snacks later.

After I took one look at the board, I gave a sigh.

GAVIN: The answer is silver. It's the only one tha—

The teacher scoffed under his breath, saying that my answer was a *lucky guess*, before he went back to his lecture. Well, I was up now anyway, so I guess it's time to just stare out the window for the next seven hours of school.

CHAPTER

2

The bell finally rang for the last time, and I packed up my bag and started to make my way home. Well, I was till I bumped into a classmate of mine. Several strands of sewing equipment fell out her bag. I quickly apologized, helping the girl pick up the fallen materials.

GAVIN: Ah, I'm sorry, my bad, still clumsy.

CLASSMATE: It's fine. Really, it's fine.

I was putting the last of the needles in her bag when I remembered something about her—this girl was new here.

GAVIN: Say you're that new girl, right? Name's Gavin, your everyday friendly face.

CLASSMATE: Friendly, but not very classy, huh? Molly.

GAVIN: I have plenty class, well, more than my brother.

MOLLY: All right then, Gavin. I'll see you around then. Don't go crashing into more people on your way home, okay?

She got back up, and something dropped out of her bag before I had the chance to grab her attention. It was just a slip of paper; it couldn't hurt to read. That's what I told myself anyway.

GAVIN: Blab, blab, blab, ice cream parlor. Wait, that opens today?! *Ah, hell yeah—*

TEACHER: Gavin, *get out of my class!*

GAVIN: *Ah*, sorry, sir I'lltakemyleaverightnow! (I'll take my leave right now!)

I ran out the classroom, continuing to bump into students left and right in my haste to go out of the school. A few people were giving me weird looks, but I didn't care. I need to go check out that ice cream place downtown and *fast*. I ran out the school doors and blitzed it to the location on the card. It was close by, so it shouldn't take too long.

Seven minutes of boring walking later

GAVIN: F-finally made it!

I was panting like a madman as I walked inside. Thankfully, there wasn't anyone really inside, minus the two workers at the counter. Now I'm mature and stuff, but I have my mini kid freakouts from time to time.

GAVIN: *No way! Look at all these flavors!* One…eight… seventeen…thirty!

I may have overreacted a small bit, but the choices were very varied. They had watermelon, double chocolate, vanilla, rocky road, supreme…

WORKER A: Hey, kid, you going to keep gawking, or are you going to buy something?

The man's monotone voice snapped me back into my right mind with the low sound of laughter that could be heard from the back of the store from someone else.

GAVIN: Oh, I'm sorry. One sec.

I already knew what I wanted, so I just went for the best choice.

GAVIN: Could I get a thing for mint chocolate chips, please.

The worker sighed as he opened the slider from his side. It gave me a good enough time to read his name tag. Rudy, a name that fits his attitude almost perfectly.

RUDY: Two fifty. Pay up.

GAVIN: Thank you.

I grabbed my ice cream and went over to sit at a window seat, with Rudy returning to the back of the store with his workmate. This ice cream tasted so good, too bad the workers sucked. There wasn't any kind of TV inside the store, so I just tried to listen to whatever those two workers were saying in the back.

RUDY: Jeez, fifth customer in and I already want to quit.

WORKER B: Then why don't you? I'm already tired of your nonstop nagging. Would be great to have some peace around here.

RUDY: I can't. Especially not after the weird stuff that happened last night. Did you hear about that news of that big weird monster thing that was seen last night? Might have to find a new apartment after that shit.

Gavin: ?!

I choked a bit on my ice cream as he said that line. I can't believe the stuff from the other day already got around so fast. I looked back down at my hands, making sure I didn't look too out of the ordinary as I took another bite from my ice cream. I mostly wish I could forget yesterday.

Two days ago

REX: Vin...Gav...wake *up*!

GAVIN: Uuuuggghhh I'm up. I'm up.

REX: You okay? What happened to you, dude? You get mugged or something?

GAVIN: Uh, no clue. A cat...a-a cat beat me up. I'm not too sure.

REX: Really? A cat? You omega suck, dude.

It must've all been a dream, I guess, or some kind of dumb prank. When I woke back up from whatever that trip was, the sun had set and turned to night. It turned out that I was passed out in the middle of the street, and Rex was the one to find me. My mom was so worried for me that the second we got home, I was bombarded with a load of questions before I was sent to my room right after. It wasn't that bad, but even after supposedly being asleep for a few hours, I felt so drowsy, hitting my bed and instantly falling back asleep. Even now I still remember how vivid and strange the dream I had was.

I was just falling in a void of darkness that felt like an eternity. When I opened my eyes, I only saw one thing: a pair of piercing yellow eyes staring back at me. I wanted to say something, anything before I felt something wrap around my neck, choking me.

The next morning I woke up to what was a new feeling. I got out of bed and noticed how much stronger I felt, mostly because I grabbed my door handle and ripped it right off its hinges. I panicked a bit and put it back on, and I quickly left for the bathroom to try and calm myself down. It was so weird 'cause the second I turned on the water in the sink, I could hear Rex from his room getting up. Now this wouldn't have startled me as much as it did if Rex's door was the furthest from the bathroom.

REX: Where is it? I put it right here?!

GAVIN: Hmm? Rex? What the—

I wasn't paying attention to the water in the sink, and it started to overflow. I panicked and tried to turn off the water, almost crushing the handle in the process. I was about to react when I slipped on the water on the floor. I grabbed onto a towel rack and ripped it out of the wall easily. I was trying my best to not panic any harder as I tried to put the rack down. I picked up the towel to clean up the water quickly, then I left the restroom, got dressed, and left the house as fast as I can. I just needed a lot of air right now. I hopped on the first train I could and hopped off at the first stop, which wasn't the best idea 'cause the first stop off this train leads to this train waste yard. It was heavily off limits to come here, but I should be fine here for just for a few minutes. It was easy to jump the fence and find a small area inside an old train just to think. For a few minutes, this did seem to work. I had a moment to just clear my mind on what just happened over the morning. I don't work out a lot but, was I getting stronger? I reached out over to a random piece of metal, and I started to bend it, snapping it clean in half. It was rusted, but it was easy. My hands didn't even feel hurt from gripping the rusted metal in the slightest. It was like magic.

GAVIN: Woooooaaaaahhhh. This is amazing! *I feel great!*

For the next few minutes, I was picking up random things of metal and bending and ripping them apart. Then I realized how fast I was running. I was like a track expert with my stamina! I was doing cartwheels and flips, just having the time of my life around the train yard. It felt great. After about an hour, I finally lay down in the middle of some broken trains and let out a hard sigh of relief.

GAVIN: O-oh man. This is…amazing. Wait till I show Rex—

My talking was cut short when a group of birds landed next to me. I didn't even move, but all of them started to attack me for no good reason. I hate birds; they're just big rats with wings. And rats aren't even that bad.

GAVIN: H-hey! Get off! I said—

The birds flew off, but I was still angry, so I jumped up and grabbed one out of the air. I was about to yell at it a bit more, but I realized I hadn't landed yet. I looked down, and I was high up in the sky and just falling—fast. I didn't even have the time to shout out, but something else caught my attention. Right before I hit the ground, I felt a strange surge of something flow around me as I landed on my…*tails*. I quickly forgot about the pain from the fall, and I started to quickly look over myself. I felt completely different, and I felt so itchy all over. When I scratched, I realized I had claws and fingerless gloves. The claws were glowing with strange yellow energy. I then really took notice of the two foxlike tails that saved my fall. I started to panic again at everything that had just suddenly changed. I ran over to a faded mirror, and I looked at the changes. I looked like some kind of human-fox thing, with big green eyes and two pointy ears that were twitching wildly. Even my clothes were different. A blue sweater with very light-feeling boots. So many things were racing through my mind, but just as suddenly it happened, it all just disappeared in a puff of black smoke.

GAVIN: What…huh? *What the fuck?!*

For the next hour, I would try to do whatever I did to get that fox thing back. Eventually, I just gave up and just sat back down in the middle of a rundown train car from before. I decided to look out the window just to watch the sun hit noon. Maybe I was just hungry and that was stopping me from using my powers. It bothered me to no end till I heard the sound of something opening. I thought I was the only one here, and I did my best to hide in the car. When I finally built the courage, I looked back out the window to see a robed figure walking around things, monsters covered in pure black. I watched as the robed figure was saying something to them. I tried to listen in, but the sound coming out of the creatures was drowning them out. The figure then turned to where I was hiding for a second, so I hid down, listening to that same opening sound from before. When I got back up, everything was gone. I thought it was over, when one of those things showed up in the cart I was hiding in. It started to make loud groaning noises, and I was petrified by its sight. My heart raced as it got closer to me, and I started to back away from it. I wanted to run, but the exit was right behind it. I wasn't thinking clearly, and in a blaze of fear and rage, it happened again. I turned into that fox and punched the thing into the back of the train car. I took the chance to run out, only to be met with more of them. The one I knocked on the train came out and bit one of my tails. I swung it around at the others. If it wasn't a fight before, it was one now. The things started to rush at me, and the best thing I could think to do was just run. Run until I can think of a better idea. Call it a thing of pride or blind stupidity, but my legs never moved. The things came at me, and I threw a punch at one of the beasts as it disappeared in a puff of smoke. I was just as surprised, then I went in to hit another, and another. Before I knew it, all of them were just gone, and I was left panting in a rage and fear with these weird shining shards in my hands.

Gavin: H-heh…How's…that…

Male Voice: *Who's there?!*

Gavin: Oh shit, run, run, run.

Someone else was getting closer to me, and I got back up to make an escape. I heard him gasp before I hopped over the fence again, running back to the train station. I heard the footsteps get closer, so I just ran alongside them until I got home.

Present

I didn't want any of that. I just want to have a normal life with my family. If anyone knew about my new powers, I could put people in danger. Worse, my family. I don't know what or who gave me these powers, but for now I just want to lie low and not do anything with them. Then, again, maybe someone gave me these powers to do good with them. These kidnappings, all the crime in this city. People need a miracle, right? I could be that miracle and help save people. Then I'm gonna do the best I can with them, and no one is gonna—

RUDY: *Hey, kid, store's closing! Get out!*

GAVIN: Oh, I'm sorry.

Well, I guess I'll figure this out later. Yeah, definitely later, after this ice cream. I pulled the shards out of my pocket and just looked at them again, then I hopped on a train to get back home. Several new ideas of how I would do good in the world popped into my mind, and I was enjoying every single one.

GAVIN: Heh, looks like my sleep schedule will be fucked for
who knows how long.

CHAPTER

3

Ah, home sweet home. After a long day of school and train riding, it's good to come back to a safe and comfy place. A two-story home that's been around way longer than even I care enough to remember. One that was passed down from one family member to the next, and for how old it seems to be, it never needed to be fixed with anything much than the average gutter check. Then again, my dad takes care of most of its problems so the rest of us don't have to worry. My father tends to overwork himself with his job at an electrical company, which is cool, but I don't want him to overwork himself for us. It really should be me doing it.

GAVIN: *Hey, Mom, I'm home!*

I walked inside, and Rex was sitting on the couch, watching TV. His gaze glazed over to me, giving a small nod before going back to watching whatever he was originally. That was the most of our interactions if we're not fighting each other. A strong smell of curry led me into the kitchen. My mom was cooking a grand meal. I guess, Mom had a great day at work 'cause this doesn't happen often. She works for some kind of company, I forget which, but when she is in a good mood, my brother and I try our best not to sour it with any bad news.

MOM: Oh, Gavin, you're home. Do you mind watching this
    for me? Need to grab something from the back.

GAVIN: Yes, ma'am.

She moved away from the pot as I got a better look at the kind of curry she was making.

GAVIN: Ah, perfect, it smells great. Wait, it's missing the
   secret ingredient. Let me just…

I reached into a small drawer, lifting up a small board to reveal a small pink bottle of substance. It was my secret ingredient that is perfect for curry. I can never let anyone in my family know how I got this, especially with how hard it is for me to grow this kind of flower. I spun the small bottle around a bit. It was still okay. I popped the vial open and quickly poured the contents in the pot, mixing it with curry, before taking a little taste.

GAVIN: Yep, there we go. That tastes way better.

With that done, I turned down the fire and went back to sit with Rex on the couch. He looked at me, giving a small head tilt as he flipped through random channels.

GAVIN: You good?

REX: Yeah.

GAVIN: Any homework?

REX: Nope.

GAVIN: Fail another test?

REX: Sixty percent on my last one.

GAVIN: Hey, that's better than that thirty last time.

REX: I guess.

GAVIN: What about that song you were working on?
   Coming along nicely?

REX: It's going. Can you stop asking me stuff already and
   just watch TV.

GAVIN: All right then. What's on?

Old cartoon reruns, boring infomercials, nature documentaries—the entire channel surf. It got to the point where he just landed on the news. It was the only thing worth watching anymore anyway with the recent strange events that were going on around town. As the news sprung to life, it started with the same old stuff. A huge list of crimes, places that have a higher crime rate, and a huge list of missing people that just seems to get longer and longer every day. The police and the news say that the victims have no real pattern or method of attack, so there was nothing that they can really do to help. It was this very reason that Rex and I aren't allowed outside anymore after dark. Now I get why Rex can't be out late. He's only eleven, but I'm almost eighteen, basically an adult. Then again, after that cat, I'm fine with staying home. Especially after yesterday with that robed figure and those black freaks. I still could hear the sound of their roars as I punched them. It creeped me out. Then something caught my attention on the news. It was just a video of a man doing the weather, but in the background, it showed those things. Rex didn't seem to notice, but I did. Everything went silent for a second, then there was an explosion. It happened right behind the reporter. The camera got cut off, and I looked wide eyed at Rex's emotionless face.

REX: That was boring, next.

GAVIN: Did you see those things in the back?!

REX: What things in the back?

GAVIN: Those black shadow things?! They atta—uh, *never mind.*

REX: Is this one of those dumb book things again?

GAVIN: No, *no!* Just turn the news back on!

When the news finally came back up, there was a big error message that was played over and over.
Our mother came in and just sighed at both of us.

MOM: Now if only you were this focused on finding a job, Gavin.

GAVIN: I-I'll find one soon, Mom, I swear.

REX: We're just watching the news and something cool happened. There was—

MOM: I don't care. Gavin, I know it's late, but I need you to run to the store again to get some milk. Think you coul—

GAVIN: *Done. Got it. Just text me the list. Bye!*

I grabbed my phone and ran as fast as I could to the train station, hopping on the first train to where the report was. I wondered why I was so invested in this, then I realized this would be my first job as a hero or something. I need to think of a name for myself.

Downtown

I hopped off the train the second I could and ran as fast as my legs would take me, right to where that news report happened. Sure enough, the building was swarmed with police, but they didn't seem to be moving or anything. They were just guarding the area. There were several people just standing around. Then a woman was dragged out.

WOMAN: *He's still in there, my son—*

POLICE: *Shut up, you saw nothing!* That gas leak—

Gas leaks, my ass, it was those things fault. I heard a lot of crashing noise coming from the side of the building that I noticed no one was really guarding. I snuck over to that side without anyone noticing me. There was an open window over on that side, letting me inside. The bottom floor seemed completely empty, the only light being the flashes of red and blue from the emergency light outside. I heard the same growls from before, and it was coming from upstairs. It shook me down to the core. I took in a deep breath and turned into that weird fox thing again, building the courage to walk closer to the sounds.

GAVIN: All right…all right…no pressure…you got this… you beat them before…kinda. *Fuck, what am I even doing here?*

As I got closer to the growls, I heard a scream of terror, which instantly put me into overdrive. I ran right to it. The screams seemed to come from this empty apartment. Those things from earlier were destroying the place, breaking dishes and photos, and eating anything

16

into their mouth. The second they noticed me, they all started to scream. I put on a brave face. These ones looked way different from the ones I beat at the train yard as these ones were like giant balls of slime. The second one bit my leg, and I punched it hard, slamming it into what was left of a kitchen. More sounds started up again, then the kitchen started to burst into flames. The things started to disappear, and they left more of those weird crystals. I wanted to try and chase them down, but I heard cries from a room in the back.

GAVIN: *Shit, shit, shit.* Not good. *Hey, who's back here?!*

I kept calling out, then someone started to scream out from a room. When I opened the door, there was a large beast attacking a closet, and there was a small kid screaming inside. It was completely on fire as it was burning the door down slowly. I grabbed the closest thing to me and grabbed its attention.

GAVIN: Hey, big, *uh…candlestick! Try this!*

Now if I was my younger brother, my insults would've been way better. But it did get the thing's attention, and it rushed right at me, tackling me to the ground. It was burning me. I couldn't get it off me, and I was screaming out in pain. When I managed to roll it off me, my new clothes were completely burned off. Then I landed a hard kick onto it. It slammed into the wall, leaving a burn mark, and it screamed out in pain. It slowly got back up and tried to rush me again. I panicked. I wanted to beat this thing, but it was completely on fire. Touching it would just burn me more. I was getting angry, then something just snapped in me. My hands glowed again, and I stood my ground right at the thing. I let out a small grunt as a beam of something shot out my hands. It completely destroyed the beast in a single blast. It felt completely normal like I knew exactly what to do.

GAVIN: Woooooah…I did that? I can do that? *Sick.*

I was about to try out and fire a random blast, but the apartment started to burn around me.

GAVIN: *Fuck, not the time to play hide-and-seek. Hey, kid, you can come out now!*

The closet opened quickly, and the kid ran right up and hugged my leg. Then he looked right up at me and screamed again. He tried to run back into the closet again, but I stopped him with one of my tails before he could hurt himself.

GAVIN: Woah, woah, woah. See, I'm cool, I'm cool. Friendly.
Those things are gone.

KID: P-please don't eat me.

GAVIN: Eat you? I'm not gonna— Never mind. Hey, I saw
your parents outside. Want me to take you to the—

The room around us started to break apart as the fire was spreading more. The kid tried to hide in his closet again, but the ceiling started to collapse. The door behind us got blocked off, and I rushed over and grabbed the kid out of the way. He looked at me completely shook out of their skin.

KID: *I…help…*

GAVIN: …

Looking around the room, I realized that the only way out was out the window. We were only on the third floor. I can make that landing, right? I just reacted and hopped out the window, falling over the side of the building. I kept the kid safe within my arms, and I landed into a garbage bin. The kid was okay, and I was less okay. Bonus points: Nothing felt broken, but trash really hurts to land on.

GAVIN: Hey, kid, you okay?

KID: Y-yes…*that was so cool!* We jumped out the window,
and we went *whoooos, and you were—*

I heard someone running closer to us. It was a woman, and she got a good look at the two of us.

WOMAN: *Aahhhh, that monster has my child.*

KID: *Mom!*

The mother ran up and grabbed her kid, then she punched me right in the face. Just then a few cops came over as well, and not even wasting a second, they tried to shoot and fire at me wildly. I panicked and made a break for it, just thankful that none of the shots hit me as I was running down more alleyways, then I hid in a safe place to turn back to normal.

GAVIN: *That…was…definitely something.*

I got a small text from my mom asking if I got the milk yet. I just let out a soft laugh, and I gave her a small text:

GAVIN: I'm okay, Mom, and I think I have a job now. See you home soon.

—m—

NEWS REPORT: This just in, after the mysterious sighting of this strange wolflike figure, several have wondered if the mysterious disappearance of many may be connected to the sightings. If you have any information about the creature, please tell the authorities. We also ask viewers to be on the lookout for strange shadowlike creatures that seemingly come out of thin air. There are suspicions that the two might be connected.

CHAPTER

4

I woke up the next day completely drained after yesterday. Last night was definitely way too much for me. All I wanted to do was to go back to sleep. You know what? It's a holiday for some guy I don't care about. I'll just...go...back to...zzzZZZ.

—⁂—

Rex walked past Gavin's room and peered inside. He was sleeping loudly and snoring hard.

REX: He must be really tired. He looks so dumb sleeping
     like that.

Rex watched him resting peacefully for a moment. He wanted to forcefully wake him up and make him breakfast, but instead, he closed the door softly. Rex walked downstairs into the living room to figure out what to do on his day off. Both his parents were out for the day, spending time with each other, and Gavin was dead asleep for who knows how long. He could play on his new console for the entire day or work his story without him being bothered by any of his family members. This was the perfect day off if there wasn't a loud knocking on the door.

REX: *Uuuuuuuugggggggghhhhhh.*

It was almost going to be a perfect day. He got up from the family couch and walked over to the front door. The knocking seemed to get faster and angrier as he got closer to the door.

Rex: All right, all right.

He opened the door almost furiously as he didn't care who was at the door He just wanted them gone so he could return to enjoying his free time.

Rex: *Who is—?*

He stopped himself as he saw a very tall and very athletic-looking woman at the door, looming over him. She was wearing glasses and had black-and-white hair. The main thing that caught Rex's attention was the deep scar on the woman's chin and neck that slightly showed off her teeth. For a moment, Rex wondered if this was a friend of his parents.

Tall woman: Huh, a kid. Wouldn't think a squirt like you would have them.

Rex: Who are you?

Tall Woman: I don't have much time, kid. So just tell me the truth and give me those crystals. Really don't wanna have to get physical this early in the day.

The woman then tried to grab Rex's head, but he smacked the hand away.

Rex: I'm sorry, but I don't know you. *Goodbye!*

He then slammed the door on her face and quickly locked it. He left the door feeling victorious, then he walked back upstairs for his guitar, tuning it a bit. He was about to start playing, trying to get in any amount of practice for the day, when there was another knock at the door. He got up and ran to the door, expecting the same person to be out there.

Rex: *Woman, for the last time—*

He opened the door to yell at her, trying to seem tough despite being only a preteen.

Rex: *Piss off.*

The tall woman standing there was gone, and in place was a girl looking around the same age as him. She looked very polite and was wearing earrings, which grabbed his attention, then he went back to looking brave.

Rex: Eh, what do you want?

Girl: I'm sorry for my mother's attitude. She was never the best *people person*.

She extended her arm out for a handshake, which wasn't reciprocated by the young boy.

Girl: Hi, my name is Akoi.

Rex: If you and your psycho mom don't leave right now, I'll have to beat you both up.

Akoi: I'd like to see you try. Anyway, we really need those shards. It's important.

Rex: Shards? Like I said before—I. Don't. Know what you're talking abo—

He then felt a very hard chop on his neck, and he quickly began to pass out. The last thing he heard were the two arguing.

Akoi: *Mom!* Why did you do that?

Tall Woman: We need to move out of here. We'll just take him with us.

Akoi: But we didn't need to—

Who knows how long later

The small kid woke up in a dark room completely confused as to where he was or how he got there. All the walls were concrete. The only way out were some stairs that ran off up into the dark. There was a sound of leaking pipe behind him, almost to taunt him, as he started to look around more. He was tied up in a chair, and he couldn't move his arms or his legs. He let out grunts, trying his best to escape. Then a sinking realization hit him. He was kidnapped. Several thought ran around his head with only three crying out the most in his head.

REX: I wanted my mom, my dad, my brother. Someone, anyone, I need help. I just want to go home. *I don't want to be here.*

To the boy's dread, as if she came from the shadows, the tall woman from earlier appeared right in front of him.

TALL WOMAN: Okay then. Answer our questions and then I'll think about it.

REX: *Just let me go already! I don't care about that! I just want to go home! Get me out of here you tall, four-eyed, zombie-faced, witch-hair kidnapper!*

TALL LADY: We'll see about that.

She grabbed his head, and he kept trying to escape from the chair. After a second, she let go, completely confused.

TALL WOMAN: That doesn't add up. But how? You really don't know anything.

REX: Oh, so now you believe me, dumbass!

TALK WOMAN: First off, my name is Telum, kid. Second off—

REX: *Does it look like I care? Just let me go!*

He tried to struggle and thrash as much as he could until the chair fell over, causing Rex to land on his face. The woman chuckled at his continued thrashing about.

TELUM: Ha-ha! Oh, you have the spirit, all right. Tell yeah what...

She leans over to his ear.

TELUM: (Whispering) If you help me and Akoi collect the shards we're after and promise not to tell anyone about us, I'll set ya free.

REX: Why should I? *You're gonna kill me!*

TELUM: Kill you? Hell, no. Why would you even think I'd do that?!

REX: Y-you're the kidnappers on the news, right?

TELUM: Would you believe me if I said that we're actually against them?

REX: *Hell, no!*

TELUM: Well, we are, and *if things go well*, you will too. Welcome to the team, kid.

She snapped her finger as the rope around him instantly loosened. The second that happened, he got up, punched her as hard as he could, and ran as fast as he could for the stairs. The woman rubbed the area where she was punched as she watched him leave.

TELUM: I'll teach ya how to throw a better punch later!

He got up the stairs and out the basement as fast as he could, searching around frantically for an exit. He ran in a random direction into what looked like a living room. He ran past a small...dragon?

DRAGON: Oh, you're leaving? Bye, Rex, see ya soon!

She opened the door for him as he burst out the front door, running past the dragon, who watched him leave with a smile. He didn't even know where he was headed until he ran into a set of very familiar arms.

GAVIN: Rex, what are you doing here?

REX: Gavin? *Gavin!*

Rex ran right into his brother, giving him the largest hug he could, to the strange discomfort of his older brother. For some reason, he smelled strongly of sea water, but it didn't bother Rex at all.

GAVIN: Uhhhhhhhhh, you feeling okay?

For a long while Rex didn't say anything, just holding his brother in a tightening dead-like hold.

GAVIN: Well, tell ya what. I was going to get some pizza. You can come with me and tell me what's wrong, okay?

REX: Deal.

On the way there, Rex tried to tell him what happened, but he just couldn't. The words literally never left his mouth. He just hoped he would never see those two ever again.

CHAPTER

5

Earlier that same morning

A loud slamming noise woke me back up from my morning nap. I really wanted to sleep longer, but I had to get up eventually. I was still groggy, letting out a long, hard yawn as I got out of bed. I looked around the house, expecting someone else to be there, but heard nothing. No Mom, no Dad, and no Rex? That's weird, but not unheard of. I bet the family went to do something without me. Wouldn't be the first time I was left behind or me saying that I wanted to stay home. I didn't have a reason to leave the house, so I planned on just staying home, making myself a sandwich and focusing on figuring out what kind of power I used yesterday. I held my hand out a window and flicked it around a bit. Nothing came out, and I sighed a bit.

GAVIN: Great, what the hell is going on with me? *I wish I had some answers or some kind of hint. Then again, who in the world could I even ask for help about this?*

I started to walk back upstairs when I accidentally knocked the table where I kept the crystals onto the floor, and they fell close to an old set of pants that I wore last night. Before I had the chance to pick them up, the crystals all started to glow brightly. I instinctively switched back into my fox form, hiding behind my bed. What if this is how those things get summoned? I can't fight these things here! After a long few seconds of anticipation, the lights started to fade, leaving a small blue crystal compass. The fox form disappeared as I looked at the compass from afar, calming back down from the sudden event.

GAVIN: All that light show for this?

I picked it up, and it opened itself up. The hand started to spin wildly for a bit before randomly pointing in a direction. It wasn't pointing north, but it was pointing somewhere. It felt so weird as I held it in my hands, like something in my chest told me that I needed to follow it. Well, I did ask for answers. Maybe this is a sign? In any case, I suddenly didn't want to stay home all day. Let's just call this my second mission. I quickly got myself dressed, and I started my mini quest of finding out where the compass would lead me. I went back to the train station to see where it would lead me.

A few minutes of train travel later

GAVIN: All right, compass, show me what I want to know.
Please.

I started walking as safely as I could for a while, following wherever the compass pointed, but it was confusing at times. It would just point in different directions almost randomly. Sometimes it would even try to put me into danger, with me almost walking down some not- pleasant streets. Maybe it was because of all the walking or the rush of the unknown, but I was getting a bit excited as to what this compass could show me. It could be where those things come from, and I could beat it right then and there. Or maybe it would show me some secret treasure! Whatever it was, the compass would lead me to it, hopefully.

It wasn't long when the compass guided me over to the port side of the downtown area. I remember hearing a bunch of classmates saying something about this place being cursed. A lot of fishermen say to avoid the water here 'cause there was no fish here. I wondered why. Walking alongside the beach line, I heard some meowing. Then I saw the same cat from before sitting by a small cave opening. It just sat and stared at me as if it was waiting for me. The compass seemed to point to the opening. I was just confused by the sight of the cat.

GAVIN: Wait, you again? Trying to steal more fish from me?

The cat looked at me hard before running away again off the beach. The compass started to shine a lot more as I stood at the cave entrance. I shrugged it off as I started to walk down the cave a bit. I heard then what sounded like a low growl come from deep inside the cave. My entire body shook as any courage I did have instantly left my body.

GAVIN: Yeah, you know what, I'm gonna go. Not today.

I turned back around, then the cool open air quickly vanished. There was a wall, leaving me locked in wherever I was. When I turned back around again, it was the same. I was trapped in a cave, and before I even had time to process all of it, the floor gave out, and I fell deep into the dark.

Within deep darkness

GAVIN: Uuuuuuugggghhh. What the hell was that? Why does the floor feel gross?

I pulled myself off the damp floor, then I realized that the floor had turned rotten and molded over wood. The air was just as salty as before, but instead of the sounds of the sea and waves crashing, it sounded like I was in a submarine going deeper underwater. I started to walk toward the closest door to me, finding out it was jammed tightly. I even tried turning into that fox form to try and bust the door down to no avail.

GAVIN: Is this way blocked or something? Come on, open up, you stupid door.

As I was ramming the door with my shoulder, the compass fell out of my pocket and rolled over to a hole in the floor, teetering on the edge. I silently walked over and grabbed it, then the floor gave out again, causing me to fall even deeper into this strange area. The sound of splashing water echoed around the room as I got back to my feet and off the wet floor. The compass, thankfully, fell a bit farther ahead of me. It was still intact, and as I reclaimed it, its blue glow started to shine brighter.

GAVIN: Ahhhh. Okay, okay, no more falling, ugh. Huh?

I was about to put it into my pocket when the case flipped wide open and the words on the inside changed completely.

"Kit…you…are…back."

It shined again just as I was finishing reading the four words, and a new set appeared for me to read.

GAVIN: "Find…me…save…me…"

It flashed again and turned back to a regular compass, then it pointed deeper into this strange place.

GAVIN: Save? Wait, I think I've heard about this somewhere.
     This is a ghost thing, right? But ghosts aren't real…*says
     the talking fox.*

I sighed as I started to walk deeper into the wooden structure. The more I walked, the more I heard those weird sounds. The area was pitch black and flooded in several areas, with several parts of the floor being broken open by what looked like teeth marks. The smell was really getting to me. It was a horrible smell of dry seaweed mixed with a humid smell of mold. I was glad that I was on a light stomach; otherwise, I might've just puked out all my guts.

I continued my way through a corridor, and I could swear something was moving in the water under me. It was getting on my nerves slightly, but they quickly faded away when I moved into a more wide open room. It had a strange statue of what seemed to be a woman, and it was standing at the center. The room didn't go on anywhere else, and I tried to find any kind of exit from here. I was about to start looking around the statue when I heard the softest voice ever telling me to jump in the water. It seemed so peaceful all of a sudden. I started to lean over an edge, and I fell into the water. I just lay on the surface, not moving an inch, then several things started to bite me. I panicked for a split second and turned to see what was biting me. Piranhas, or some kind of fish that looked like them, were biting away at my clothing. I swam as fast as I could to the top of the wood, panting crazily. Then I started to pat myself to make sure no other fish was over me from my quick underwater trip.

GAVIN: *Aaaaaaaaaaaahhhh*…fuck. What the fuck. Ah, aahhhh, fuck. I'm okay. I can breathe.

As I got back out, I heard laughing coming from somewhere. I tried to pinpoint where it was coming from. I shook myself off as I pulled out my phone from my pocket.

GAVIN: Still good. These things are invincible.

VOICE: So you ignore me now.

The strange voice seemed clearer now. The statute itself was talking. I backed up a bit as the voice continued.

STATUE: Oh, you men are all so easy to lure. Why didn't you just let my pets finish you off easily? We've been hungry for sooooooo long.

GAVIN: A…a talking statue? I'm not dreaming, right?

STATUE: Wait, you again? No, no. *You should've died in that wave! Die, die, die.*

The room started to shake wildly as several sharp teeth started to burst from the floor around where I was standing. I hopped out the way. They turned to splinters as the wood underneath me gave way. I saw several piranhas just eating away at the wood within seconds. The statue kept screaming over and over, and the water underneath me started to shoot out the piranhas right out the water like homing missiles. I tried my best to move out of the way as the statue just kept screaming "Die" over and over. It was so annoying, hearing the screaming over and over, annoying me to no end that it wouldn't just shut up. It was then that I slightly noticed that anywhere I would step, the statue would move all their attention there. That gave me a great plan. The second I got a clear chance, I ran right up to the statue and screamed even louder as a wave of water appeared right where it stood. With one last dodge, the statue hit itself out of the area and into the dark depths of the water.

GAVIN: H-he, he-he. *Ha, I win!* I did it. I did it. I—

The wood started to shake more, and the wood broke into small planks, pulling me deeper into the water. All I could see while submerged was the remains of the statue. Then the piranhas all started to swim right to me. I tried to swim back up, and my hands started to lightly glow a bit. The piranhas had started to bite into my legs before I could get out. The statue started laughing, being drowned out by the water. I was getting bitten more and more, and I was running out of air quickly. I remembered the last time my hands glowed like this and put faith into the attack as I put my hands together. It felt like something was changing in my hands, and I aimed right for the statue. I released a large beam of energy, fired right from my hands. It jetted me right out the water and destroyed the statue, and the piranhas all started to fade away.

The room finally went silent when I returned from the water. I saw a door that wasn't there before, and I figured that it was where I needed to go. I coughed up a bit of water and sat still next to a wall. I'm just gonna rest here a bit, then walk through it. I think I was still breathing. My heart was pounding heavily as I got up and shook off the pain in my legs. Then the compass lit up again.

GAVIN: "Good…job…keep…going." Are you *trying* to get me killed? I just want to go home.

It shined one last time, and the doors opened wide into the dark depths.

GAVIN: "So…close…help…me." All right, Mr. Spirit, let's go then.

CHAPTER

6

Past the door was yet another long hallway, with the same sounds from before being my only real source of comfort. This time the area felt more fixed as the floors looked more stable to walk on. Before I realized it, my eyes had finally adjusted to the darkness. I was glad that I wasn't walking in basically pure darkness, and I prayed on luck to help me guide my way. After falling in the water several times before, I tried to open my flip phone, praying that it would still work. To my surprise, it booted to life almost flawlessly. Even if there was no signal, it helped me calm down a bit after that statue from earlier. As I walked further in this strange place, I slowly started to guess where I could be. I started getting anxious of what could be ahead of me. I was so distracted by my own thoughts that I didn't notice a giant door in front of me.

GAVIN: Woah, this is huge. Almost like its sealing something inside.

I hesitated for a second as I felt my heart sink again. I took one last deep breath to build up my courage, then I put a hand on the door.

GAVIN: All right, what's behind door number one?

I pushed open the door and saw nothing. It was a wide-open area that held nothing.

GAVIN: Huh? I guess I got overhyped for nothing.

I took a few steps inside, then looked around the place. The entire room was an underwater sea dome. It had this bright light at the center of the room. As I was walking to the center, I looked around at the windows. Then I saw the coolest thing ever: fish everywhere, some with strange patterns that I've never seen on a sea creature before. I just stared at all of them moving along outside, just living all together. I kept looking around, then I spotted a small hole alongside one of the windows. It looked like it could fit the compass, so I walked over to the hole and placed the compass inside. It shined brightly, then something sounded like it was unlocking underneath my feet. An opening in the floor started to creek open with a loud rumbling, causing all the fish around the area to leave in a hurry. It was ominous, but nothing to be concerned about, right? I started to look around the glass more, then a large creature zoomed by the window. It was too dark and fast for me to see what it was, but it was definitely huge. Then the center part of the room that had opened up started to bubble furiously, like it was boiling. I stepped away from it as something came bursting from the depths. One...two...several tentacles. Now I've read enough books to know getting caught by those is a bad idea. I started to move back as more started to pull out of the water. The room started to fill with them, and the tentacles all started to try and grab me. I did my best to dodge them all and managed to slice at one with my claws. The second I did it, the tentacle pulled away, and the rumbling started again. When the rumbling stopped, a large squid-like beast showed its head. It was a sea monster otherwise known as...

GAVIN: *A fucking kraken?! Are you kidding me?!*

It let out a mighty roar as it started to slam all its tentacles directly for me and tried to grab me with all its might. I just kept dodging with no real direction to the kraken's monster roaring. It was getting angrier as I would avoid and evade all its strikes. Eventually, one landed at the glass, cracking it a bit. I realized that if the glass broke, then I would have to swim all the way back to the surface with this thing after me.

GAVIN: Oh no! *Hey, quit it!*

It paid no attention to my yelling, slamming its head into the glass, cracking it a bit more. This made this already stressful fight on a very soft time limit. But that really didn't bother me as much because I was doing nothing to it. I couldn't get enough time to focus on my hits.

Any hit I would do barely did anything to its skin. If anything, I was just annoying the kraken, which was swinging more tentacles at me. I guess it knew that too 'cause it stopped focusing on me and kept trying to break the glass. I was at a loss of what to do. I looked around to see if I could use anything to help; but the only things in the room were me, the kraken, and the blue compass in the wall. With no better options, I made a mad dash to the compass and tried to open it while it was stuck in the wall. With some luck, it popped open and gave me a great advice.

GAVIN: "Hit…the…floor…button…" Okay, but *what floor button*!

My panicking wasn't helped by the fact the kraken had just broken the glass wide open and water was pouring rapidly into the room. I swore that after it did that, it looked at me as if to say, *"Fuck you."* I started running around the place, just hoping to hit the button by accident, as the water kept rushing in. The kraken was still slamming its tentacles at me while this was all happening on the opposite side of the room. I dodged a few until I slipped on the wet floor. It gave the chance to grab my leg and started flinging me all over the place. Call it luck but it slammed me right next to the button, but before I could hit it, the kraken lifted me up into another slam. It slammed me one last time into the cold water floor. I didn't care about the pain. I quickly got back up and made a break for the button. The kraken grabbed my leg again, but this time, I hit the button first. A loud alarm sounded off, and the entire roof popped wide open, leaving me to hold my breath for a moment and accept my fate. I thought it was over, but then the ground started to quickly rise back to the surface of the water and high into the air. I swore I heard a cracking sound like glass as I floated in the air a bit. I realized this was my only chance to win, so I put my hands together, aimed at the sky, and shouted something I made up on the spot for the weird aura.

GAVIN: *Fox fire!*

I fired the beam from earlier, and it propelled me right into the kraken and slamming me into the water hard. Then I grabbed onto a piece of floating wood. The kraken floated for a second on the surface of the water, completely confused. I noticed its beak was broken. Not wasting another second, I charged the attack again and fired as hard as I could at the kraken dead on. I heard it cry out in pain.

GAVIN: Man, I almost feel bad for it. Almost.

The kraken started to fade away in a puff of black smoke, and it sank back to the sea, leaving me on the small planks of wood. I had won, *again*! I felt like a complete badass after it. As I was about to make a victory cry, something came right out the water, scaring the victory out of me. It was blue, just like the compass, so I think this was the thing that needed my help. It floated down to me and started talking to me, but after everything today, I have the right to defensively start charging another fox fire in self-defense.

BLUE SPIRIT: Thank you for rescuing m—

GAVIN: Are you trying to kill me?

BLUE SPIRIT: No, not that I would want to. But wait a second. You're not the person I thought you were.

GAVIN: Wait, what?

BLUE SPIRIT: You looked like a friend of mine. Oh no, my friends. They all are still trapped. H-hey, I need to—

GAVIN: I'm gonna stop you right there. Who are you, and who are your friends?

BLUE SPIRIT: There were four of us. We were sealed away by...*something*. I can't really remember. You heard my cries for help, and...I think you can help others too. Please, I need to save them, but I don't think I'm able to do it myself.

I shook myself off for a moment and thought. I did want answers to what was going on. Maybe saving these guys could lend me more.

GAVIN: That sounds easy enough. I just have two questions of my own.

BLUE SPIRIT: Thank you. What is it that you ask?

GAVIN: Well, one, there are these things that have shown up. Weird black creatures. Do you know anything about that?

BLUE SPIRIT: Black creatures? The shadows?! Oh no, have they not been dealt with yet? Then...*they failed.*

GAVIN: Shadows? Is that what they're really called?

BLUE: They are evil spirits that formed from an old dark god. I dealt with all of it before with my friends. Have you not dealt with them on a regular basis? I figured that you would if you've seen them.

GAVIN: No, I just started to deal with them.

BLUE: So they have returned?! That means they—yes, oh, that Kitsune didn't disappoint after all.

GAVIN: Uh, okay, and as for two, you think you could do something to help me get over there?

I pointed over in the distance to the port. I don't want to spend the next few hours paddling or swimming over it, so I wanted to just do this thing. I had a hunch it could help out in a way.

BLUE: Hmmm, I'll see what I can do. From now on, I'll be keeping an eye out for you.

The spirit then disappeared, leaving me alone on the wood, stranded in the middle of the sea.

GAVIN: Welp, guess I'm on my own to get back to the shore.

I was about to get swimming when I noticed a gigantic wave crash into the wood, pushing it toward the shore. It was so cool and so terrifying that I didn't know if I was screaming happily or scarily, but I made it back to shore in record time. By the time I got back on land, it was sunset, so nobody was on the beach. I turned back into a human and just chilled for a second.

GAVIN: What a day. I've had enough of the sea for a while.

My stomach growled loudly as I started to walk off the shore.

GAVIN: I should go get some pizza. Yeah, pizza sounds nice right now.

I got up from the sand, letting out a small groan as I did, and started walking to the closest pizza parlor. Then I heard the panting of someone familiar.

GAVIN: Rex?

What was he doing here? I could've sworn that he was with mom and dad for the day with everyone being gone from the house. He came and tackled me into a hug, leaving me confused as he usually never likes hugs.

GAVIN: Uhhhhhhhhh, you feeling okay?

He didn't say anything. It was really creeping me out.

GAVIN: We'll tell ya what. I was going to get some pizza. You can come with me and tell me what's wrong, okay?

REX: Deal.

He never did tell me what was wrong while we ate, but we did enjoy some good pizza together before heading home, and really, this was all I needed after today. Funny enough, the pizza place had a special going on for sardines on any pizza free, but I think I had enough sea food for at least a good month.

CHAPTER

7

GAVIN: You know, Rex, you still didn't tell me what got you all worked up. You sure you're okay?

REX: Y-yeah, I'm okay.

The two of us were walking home from our pizza break. I don't know why he won't tell me, especially if it was bothering him this much, but I'm too tired from today to really care. His day can't have been as tiring as mine.

Rex: So what did you do today?

Gavin: Uh, fishing?

REX: Fishing? You don't even own a boat. I can't imagine you having the guts to ask someone to borrow theirs.

GAVIN: Says you. You talk all high and mighty when you're with me, but the second someone asks you to speak in front of a crowd, you panic like a—

REX: *No, I don't.*

GAVIN: Yes, you do. May I remind you of your third-grade play where you only had a single line, and you just—

REX: *Stop talking!*

Rex then pushed me slightly in a mini. It was funny really; he always gets flustered whenever I bring up that moment.

GAVIN: Then make me, *Mr. Stagefright.*

I bopped him on the head and started running ahead of him. I looked back at him, slightly taunting him on to chase after me.

GAVIN: Tag, you're it!

The two of us started running home. I really needed this after today. I looked back as I was running, and Rex was finally smiling, chasing after me.

REX: I'm gonna—

GAVIN: Gonna what? Guess I'll never find out unless you
    catch uuuuuppp!

REX: *Then stop running so fast!*

The two of us raced home, forgetting all our worries.

We finally got home as night started to fall. We both knew that as we got inside and saw our parents sitting coldly at the entrance.

MOM: *And where have you two been! We were—*

This only usually happens to Rex, but recently, both of us have been getting this talk. It always hurts to get yelled at. I'd say it feels worse than the slams from the kraken. After the absolutely devastating talk with our mother, I went into my room to make a small outline of things that I knew about my current situation.

GAVIN: Okay, so I got powers from somewhere, at the
    same time the shadows appeared. If I beat them, they
    drop these weird shards. If I get enough, they create a
    compass. That compass leads to a spirit that was locked
    away. Okay, so that leaves a few questions. But that's for
    later to worry about. Also the Blue Spirit from earlier.
    I guess that means anytime those shadows show up, I
    should make it a top priority. But they haven't shown
    up in the past few days. I guess I should just rest for the
    time being.

My parents had already gone to bed, leaving Rex and me awake to sneak downstairs and watch the TV. He was channel surfing again as I sat with him just to see what was on. That was until Rex switched over to the news again.

TV Reporter: B-breaking news! *These things are a-attacking downtown!*

Gavin: No way. *I just wanna rest today.*

Reporter: What is it, Chet? Oh, thank god, the police are at the scene as—

My brother turned off the TV, then yawned a bit.

Rex: That is boring.

Gavin: Well, I'm going to bed. Good night, Rex!

I left Rex at the couch as I ran back to my room, quickly locking the door. I sat down on my bed and thought about it for a second. I just got back after that kraken today. Do I really have to? I thought about the last time I ran in head first and how I saved that one kid. I'm not gonna let that happen to anyone else.

Gavin: Fuck it! I'm going!

I hopped out my window, turning back into a kitsune. I ran back to the train station and hoped onto a train that was heading in the direction. My heart started to race again.

Gavin: Okay, okay. I can do this!

I hopped off the train earlier and used the top of the building to make my way to the sound of the commotion. It was genuinely terrifying from what I was looking at. Several shadows were everywhere, attacking people everywhere. I couldn't move for a second as I just watched.

Gavin: What would I even do here? Help the people? Stop the shadows? Leave some for the police?

The building I was on started to shake as a giant shadow like a bull started ramming it over and over, trying to knock it down. I fell from the building, landing hard on the beast's neck. It fell silent for a bit.

Gavin: Ahhhh, that hurt. Great, now I'm down here—

I heard a woman scream at me, then a few cops started to pull their attention away from the shadows and at me. I dodged the bullets as best

I could till the giant beast grabbed all our attention. It started to dig its feet into the ground, and I realized it had multiple eyes. This gave me a quick plan as it charged at the pile of us. I hopped up on top of its horns and managed to slam it into one of its eyes, causing it to drift out of the crowd. The bull threw me off into a group of flying shadows as more shadows showed up around the place. I was starting to panic more and more as the chaos roared around me. I can't help everyone. I need help and help badly. But I was alone, and I had to do this. I decided to leave the bull to itself as I rushed around as many buildings as I could, dealing with as many of the smaller ones as I could before shifting my attention back at the bull, keeping it away from people. But the balancing act was taking its toll as I couldn't balance all three: fighting the smaller shadows, keeping the bull away, and getting people to safety. It also didn't fucking help that every person just kept screaming at me, leaving me to almost get shot several times. I did find out that like this I'm bulletproof, but not in a fun way. I couldn't keep the act together after getting shot in the face, being distracted long enough for the bull to ram into a building, causing someone to fall out a broken window.

GAVIN: *No, wait, wait, wait!*

I ran over to the person knowing that I couldn't make it in time. I closed my eyes, thinking how badly I messed up. Then all of a sudden some kind of guy grabbed her right out of midair, placing her on the ground softly. The guy then shot balls of fire at the remaining shadows, just leaving the bull. I was completely bewildered at the power in the shots of fire that when I focused back at the bull, a strong bolt of lightning pierced right through its neck, instantly turning it into smoke. A second guy ran over to the other as their attention turned to me.

LIGHTNING: Hey, you missed one. What, too busy with—

FIRE: Shut up. Just let me finish things up, Fulting.

GAVIN: What the hell… Wait, finish up?

The fire guy started to shoot fireballs at my feet as I snapped out of my amazement.

GAVIN: *Hey, hey, what's the big deal? I'm not one of those things?!*

FIRE: Huh, this one can talk. Well, let's get this one out the way.

I made a break for it, picking up as many shards as I could before the flame person rushed me out of the area. It was terrifying as I was running for my life around alleyways with the fire guy chasing me. Then I reached a dead end. I quickly looked around. Then I heard him getting closer to me. My mind started to race wildly, then I found a perfect place to hide. I popped open a sewage grate and made a quick escape, falling down into the sewers. I thought I found a safe place to pop back out. I looked around to the sight of a TV playing the news. I would've just went back down, but the news was playing about the recent carnage happening downtown.

REPORTER: After the strange attack of the strange creatures, many have wondered of the whereabouts of the three strange heroes that saved the downtown area, but many have speculated that due to the its nature, the foxlike creature that was seen is the cause of the attack. If you have any information given about the fox, please tell local informants of the monster.

GAVIN: Monster?! But all I've done is help, right? No, you know what?! Fuck that I'm gonna show this place what a real hero looks like! *I'm gonna stop every bad guy here and be a real hero!*

With my new resolve, I made my way back home, sneaked into my room, and hit my bed hard. A lot happened today, and I have school in the morning. The last thing I thought about before I fully fell asleep...

GAVIN: Who the hell were those two other guys there? Maybe one of these days...I could... zzzz...

CHAPTER

8

FULTING: Look, I'm just saying, Lighter, if you had dealt with that thing and let me go after that lady, then maybe that *fox thing* wouldn't have gotten away.

LIGHTER: Shut it. I'm not in the mood right now. Let's just get this meeting over with so I can go to bed already.

The two young men were walking down an empty hall, passing several doors that had warning labels plastered over all of them. One of the boys, named Lighter, was covered in flames that covered his legs and arms. Even his entire head was engulfed in flames. Silver hand bands locked his wrist and ankles. He was wearing what could be best described as an armored vest. The other, whose name was most likely Fulting, was dressed in a long trench coat of sorts. A mask and helmet covered his face, leaving only his eyes to be his only noticeable features. The two walked into a room and sat down at a long table silently, as if they were waiting for someone. That was till Fulting broke the silence with his stomach growling.

FULTING: Man, I hope that boss guy brings over some good grub. All that fighting stuff made me hungry.

LIGHTER: God, for five minutes, *can you just shut up?!*

FULTING: Jeez, we're teammates, remember? We have to get along.

Lighter let out a long sigh, putting his hands over his face, before sitting more upright in his chair and forcefully putting on a calm face.

LIGHTER: Fine, you're right, I'm sorry. Did you at the very
    least bring the shards those things dropped?

FULTING: You know it—

He was cut off as another door was opened from the opposite side of the room, and two more people walked in. One was a person in a business attire that looked completely different from the two sitting down, while the other was wearing a kind of armor with a very noticeable red hat and mask covering their face. They sat down with the other two. The man in the business suit walked over to the end of the table as he spoke in a very monotone voice.

MAN: So you two, how was your first outing?

LIGHTER: It was good, sir. Nothing to write home about.

FULTING: Nothing to write home about? *We were awesome
    down there!* But I do have to admit, *we should've gotten
    there faster.*

MAN: And that's what I wanted to talk to you two about
    and why this one is right there. You three are very lucky
    individuals. As you know or have figured out by now,
    this isn't a normal company. While our show front is to
    provide energy to the public, our real goal is to protect
    it from those monsters you both fought. Now then I'd
    like you two to both meet your new coworker. Introduce
    yourself and make your way back to your living quarters
    as a group. That is all I have for you today, unless you
    brought us more shards?

FULTING: Sure thing, Mr. Eugene! Heads up!

He threw the man a few shards as the man named Eugene swiftly caught them. Then he took his leave, nodding at the gesture.

EUGENE: Now if you'll excuse me, this company isn't going
    to run itself. All this work. *So little time left...*

He left, leaving the three alone in the room. For a second, no one said anything, then Lighter turned to the new person.

LIGHTER: Did you tell them your real name?

The person shook their head no as the two gave a sigh of relief. Lighter turned to Fulting as they both gave a nod.

FULTING: Yep, there's no cameras or anything in here. So that means we can all actually talk normally here. You know, originally, I said we should meet up in a supply closet. But this guy said it was stupid.

The new recruit looked confused as the other two turned off their powers to show off their real appearances. Following along, the recruit did the same.

LIGHTER: Let me guess, you were the third guy caught in that explosion, right?

FULTING: And got powers like us?

The recruit nodded happily, giving off a confident smile.

FULTING: Hey, you don't need to be all serious like this guy right here. When we're not in any training stuff or out in the field, we can use our real names and stuff. Names Max, and it's finally great to have someone else here. *Spending three days with this guy is beyond boring.*

LIGHTER: Zack, pull your weight, do as I say, and we'll get along nicely.

The recruit nodded slowly as they took in all the information, leaving the two men waiting for their introduction.

MAX: So what's your name? Are ya shy or something?

The recruit sighed a bit as they made some figures in their hand, leading Zack to catch on.

ZACK: Oh, you're mute? That just *fucking* great. First, this guy who won't shut up and you who can't say anything. *Just fucking great.*

MAX: So you can't talk at all? Then what should we call you?

They were about to show them their hat with their name written on the inside when Max jumped to conclusion, cutting off any real sign of communication.

MAX: Red hat? Oh, we could call you RH. It's a perfect
    code name and real name! Ha, I'm a genius!

RH just sighed and gave Max a thumbs-up as their stomach started to growl.

MAX: Oh, looks like someone is hungry.

RH nodded as they pulled out three small cups of instant ramen to the delight of Max and slight annoyance of Zack.

MAX: *Aw, hell ya!* Hey, let's get these back to our living area
    and chow down. You're gonna love it. Don't worry about
    space. I've lived with plenty of guys before, so one more
    isn't that bad.

RH gave a small smile at Max's enthusiasm as Max turned his powers back on as he left the room leaving RH with Zack. They were about to go join Max when Zack stopped them for a second.

ZACK: *Hey, just between the two of us. You're kind of pretty for a
    girl. Pretty obvious that you want to keep it a secret. I won't
    tell anyone. Do a good job and stay in line.*

RH took a mini step back at the comment before putting their mask back on and covering it with their mask. Internally, they talked to themselves.

RH: *He knew. How?! I look enough like a guy. I know I do.
    How did he know?*

Their thoughts were cut short as Zack turned his powers back on as he started to direct RH to their room.

LIGHTER: Come on. Meetings over. We'll get to know each
    other better some other time.

They all walked down a hall, passing Eugene, who was deep in a conversation. None of them knew the conversation he had.

EUGENE: Don't worry. Those three will do just nicely. I'm sure that they will deal with the kitsune sooner or later. We have nothing to fear, our plans will be fulfilled soon. Just be patient.

CHAPTER

9

News Reporter: I can't believe I'm actually allowed to say this on air. Over the past three days since those strange black creatures attacked our city, the crime rate has been diminishing severely. M-many well-known and previously hard-to-find criminals have been tracked down by a mysterious vigilante calling themselves the *Fox Vigilante*. In more recent news, the weather seems to be bright for the future as the next few days seem to be nothing but sunshine.

Gavin: There we go, now that's more like it.

Molly: *Gavin, the train is almost here. Let's go already!*

Gavin: *Coming!*

It's been a few days, and everything has been going great! After the news called me a monster, I got to work. During the day, I would take some time to just walk around some areas that people were known to do shady activities and just look around, sitting in some places; and I would let people talk. You'd be surprised how much people say when you have strong hearing. Using that information, I would hunt down these criminals or escapees and just blitz them with my strength. It's more sad than hard really, with how little they put up a fight. There also hasn't been a shadow attack during those days, so this could help me *train* in a way.

That aside, I decided to hang out with Molly today after school, heading off to the library to study for some test. Well, she was mostly studying as I got sidetracked looking at a book about foxes. It turns out I was a special kind of fox called a kitsune. The old book talked about them being tricksters and them being very rare, with strange powers too! I took the book home for as long as I could so I could learn as much as I could about this.

The two of us hopped onto a train and started a small talk while we rode to her stop.

MOLLY: Hey, thanks again for coming with me. I just find that place soooooo boring.

GAVIN: Yeah, I get that. Books can be boring, but sometimes they have some cool stuff in here like look at this! "Kitsunes can produce this energy called aura that they can manipulate into tools they use for trickery or helpfulness." There is even a legend here about the fox goddess called Seishin where—

MOLLY: *Uh-huh, yeah, very interesting.* I'm more into *action* and the thrill of being free, but my old hag of a grandmother is forcing me to be a doctor because, and I quote, *"It's not very ladylike of me to be outdoors."* I mean, it's still kinda cool that I know how to sew a bit, but it's not me, you know.

GAVIN: Well, why don't you become like a nursing cop? They get a lot of action right?

MOLLY: Oh naw, I could never. Especially with all that weird monster stuff and that fox, kitsune, whatever thing, running around. Oh, that reminds me. Did you hear about those three strange heroes? There's a rumor going around that there are three superheroes or something that want to go after that fox and stuff.

GAVIN: T-there is? Why? I mean that fox guy hasn't done anything wrong from what I've heard. So maybe they don't need to fight it?

MOLLY: I guess. But if I ever see that thing, I'm gonna punch its face a new one!

GAVIN: Sure, *sure*. You could try.

The train stopped, and Molly got up and waved goodbye to me with a smile. I feel so happy to have her as a friend, a real one, I mean. That's because the second she left, a small blue light that only I could see popped up in front of my face.

BLUE: Any news of the shadows?

GAVIN: Sorry, not yet, Blue.

BLUE: *Okay, thanks.*

GAVIN: Hey, cheer up, okay? I promised that I would save them, and I'll keep it.

The spirit sighed as he floated back into my sweater pocket. Blue, as I call him, has been helping me ever since I saved him, teaching me about how to better control my new powers. He even helped me name the fox fire that I used against the kraken before. The sad thing is that he has amnesia and can't remember a lot of his past. He knows that his friends are in danger, and he knows that something bad happens if these shadows aren't dealt with quickly. He says that maybe his memories will come back to him if he stayed with me, and I didn't really have a say in whether or not he could stay. It doesn't really bother me 'cause he seems so excited by the world and every little thing, especially by the lamp at my bedside.

The train slowed down in my area, and as I hopped off, a tall-looking woman and a small girl walked past me. For a moment, me and the girl locked eyes, and I swore if we were left any longer together, then...never mind.

I walked back home and was met by the sight of my family eating dinner without me. My dad works for a rival energy company at that dumb Relico place, so he's rarely ever home. I made myself a plate as I joined the table eating dinner. Rex looked just as shaken as he did when we had pizza a few days back, but I didn't bother him with it. The usual conversations happened at dinner: *How was your day? Are you keeping up your grades?* It may be because I'm more adapted at multitasking, but I've been doing my homework even faster than usual. Dinner seemed to pass by, and before I knew it, it was patrolling time! I hopped out my window like the last three nights and started my search for criminals tonight.

BLUE: So who are you looking for tonight?

GAVIN: No one in particular, maybe just stop some more petty crimes tonight. Oh hey, look down there!

I pointed down at these two men hijacking a car. From my vantage point above the building, I decided to wait a bit to make my entrance.

CRIMINAL 1: Hey, idiot, hurry up.

CRIMINAL 2: Why? We got all the time in the world.

CRIMINAL 1: Didn't you hear? That wolf guy from a few weeks ago is not coming after us now.

CRIMINAL 2: That guy? *Pfft*, they're just some guy in a kids costume. I'll tell yeah what? I bet those videos of 'em hopping shooting laser or what not is all just smoke and mirrors.

CRIMINAL 1: You think so?

CRIMINAL 2: Think so? I know so. The guy is just a faggot, a furry faggot. *Ha, a fur-fag!*

CRIMINAL 1: *Yeah!* A fur—ha-ha.

Gavin: He he he, that's a good one. You should've been a stand-up comedian with jokes like that.

The two criminals looked back and saw me just sitting above them on a ladder railing. I gave a small wave before giving a cheeky smile.

GAVIN: Wonderful night we're having, huh?

The two criminals both screamed in terror at the sudden sight of me. They both reached for their guns as I just blitz rushed the two of them. They were both knocked out cold, and I started to drag them out into the open, tying them up onto a sign.

GAVIN: Annnd there. Night, night. How was that for some smoke and mirrors?

BLUE: Good job. You're getting very fast with your movements.

GAVIN: Thanks. All righty then, all done here. On to more waiting.

I made my way back to the top of a building, and I started to wander around in the darkness of the night, trying to find any more small crimes to pass some time. I found a desolate building and sat down and just rested a bit, closing my eyes. I almost fell asleep. It was such a peaceful night that I was stargazing a bit. I wish there was less of the city light so I could see more of them. I blinked slowly one last time before I saw something. A shooting star, I guess, getting closer to me. Then a hard smell of smoke hit my nose, fully waking me up.

GAVIN: Wait, that's...*what the fuck!?*

I managed to just barely move my head out the way as a ball of fire rushed right past it, slamming on the wall behind me. I looked at the direction it came. It came from the fire guy from a few nights ago. He was floating in the air with his arms crossed.

LIGHTER: Damn, you're a quick one. Just stand still you, stupid—

GAVIN: *The hell dude?!* I didn't even do anything.

LIGHTER: So I wasn't crazy, you can talk. Hey, tell me where do you things come from, or hell, take me to your boss so I can kick its ass!

GAVIN: Wait, you mean the shadows? I told you before, I ain't one of them! I have no clue where the hell they come from. I just want to help people!

I started to get back on to my feet and took a few steps back. This guy looked so angry at me. Also, he was flying. If I wasn't so focused on not getting burned alive, I would be so excited to just gawk at how that works.

LIGHTER: Oh, so you're trying to be some kind of vigilante or something? Trying to clear your name or something so you can do more crimes then? Actually, don't answer that, it won't matter anyway.

The guy started to charge another ball of fire toward me. I made a break over the building, hopping over to the next over as the chase started. Building after building, he chased after me. I ran as fast as I could as he fired balls of fire at my feet, trying to burn them to the ground. I debated for a second on fighting back, but what Molly said on the train rang out. If these guys are good, then I shouldn't fight back. I just need to find a way to—

LIGHTER: *Got ya, you dumbass!*

He fired a large ball of fire, launching me off the building I was hoping to. I guess we had ran pretty far 'cause I landed on sand. We were back at the pier again. I was about to pull myself up, spitting out sand from my mouth, when I saw him stand high above me, pointing out a finger like a gun.

LIGHTER: So long, bitch. Snap spark.

He fired a small flame that grew bigger than I could dodge. I wanted to move, but it was coming at me so fast. I just panicked as I fired a small blast at the sand to take most of the hit for me. The ball caused an explosion, further burying me in the sand. For a minute, I stayed still and held my breath. I waited for what seemed like hours before I heard him talking to someone. Was he on a phone?

LIGHTER: Fulting, I know. I'm coming back. Great news,
the fox thing is gone. But it didn't drop any crystals. Be
back at the base soon.

He hung up, and I heard him fly off. I popped my head out the sand, coughing a bit as I watched him fly away in the distance. Blue showed back up as I was dusting myself off. Thankfully, the only thing that was hurt were the burn marks on my cloths.

BLUE: Wait, you heard that? They're after the shards too.

GAVIN: I'm a bit worried about that too. B-but don't worry,
I'll think of something.

BLUE: Say, you look very tired. You should rest. It's important
for the body.

GAVIN: I will, I will. Jeez, you're not my mom, Blue.

I let out a small laugh as I made my way back home for the night. Tomorrow will be a new day after all. Before I fell asleep, I knocked over my table as some of the shards I had from earlier fall over. I grabbed them and placed them in my backpack for safekeepings before Blue started to talk about it. He was so paranoid about things happening. I guess it couldn't hurt for me to be less lax too.

CHAPTER

10

As the older brother silently moved back into his room, his younger brother was sitting in his bed holding on to his guitar tightly from the events that happened earlier today. The day started out like any other. He woke up, used the restroom to brush his teeth, then walked downstairs to his brother, who was making breakfast for him. They ate together before they made their way to school, on the trains as usual.

GAVIN: Hey, you'll be okay walking home today? I'm going
to the library with Molly after school.

REX: Who's Molly?

GAVIN: A friend of mine.

REX: You have friends? That's a first. Also that is a girl's
name. *Do you have a guuuuuuuuurrrrrrrrlllll*friend?

The brother blushed a bit before pushing him a bit.

GAVIN: We're just friends! Besides, relationships are gross.

REX: You're gross.

The train stopped, and they both made their separate ways.

The day went by, and Rex walked home by himself. He opened the door happily and greeted his mother loudly.

REX: *Mom, I'm ho—*

He stopped himself as he saw the woman who kidnapped him so many days before sharing tea with his mother.

TELUM: Ah, so he finally shows up. He's a sweet kid.

MOM: Hello, Rex, this is Ms. Telum, your new tutor that's here to help you with your studies.

For a moment he couldn't say anything as he just stared at Telum from the doorway. His mother yelled at him a bit to close the door and sit down to talk. He did so, sitting as far away from the witch as he could. Just as he did, his mother got up to make more tea, leaving the two of them in the room alone. Rex got a better look at the woman and her very noticeable scar on her lower chin. Telum leaned forward a bit, and he inched back into his seat.

TELUM: Look, I know that we didn't start off on the *best first impression*—

REX: What are you doing in my house?

The boy grabbed the closest thing to him in an attempt to look brave in any way he could despite his size disadvantage. Telum looked at Rex with a smile, letting out a chuckle, moving her finger in a motion as the item he grabbed was ripped out of his hands and gently placed back where he got it from. It was like a magic trick to the young boy.

TELUM: Look, I'm pretty sure you have seen all the news about the shadows and that weird kitsune thing. Besides the point.

REX: Yeah, and what does that have to do about this?

TELUM: Well, me and Akoi are slightly kinda the cause of it.

REX: I didn't ask about those things or who did what. I asked why you're in my house?

TELUM: Isn't it obvious, you troglodyte. I want your help.

REX: *And why would you need my help, you*—

MOM: *Rex, be quiet!*

Telum began to laugh at the interaction with Rex, who continued his facade to look brave even if she wasn't taking him seriously. She then gave a sigh as the air felt more tense around Rex.

TELUM: Anyway, because you saw me and Akoi, you don't really have a choice. You are gonna be joining our little group.

REX: S-so you're not trying to hurt me?

TELUM: Not entirely.

REX: But why me?

TELUM: Akoi had a vision to go here for some reason. I will never doubt that girl. She's very special.

REX: So you want me, a kid, to fight those things? How would I even?

TELUM: You'll find out soon. Call it our first outing as a group.

Rex's mother finally came back from the kitchen with some tea for the two of them. Rex sat back down shrimp-ishly.

MOM: It seems you two got more comfortable.

Telum grabbed the tea and quickly finished the cup, then got ready to leave.

TELUM: Thank you, miss. I think your son here will be perfect for my tutoring. I'll see what I can do with him. I'd love to talk more, but I don't want to keep my child alone for too long. Oh and, Rex, our first lesson will be tomorrow.

She laughed a bit more before walking out the door, leaving Rex and his mother alone. Before his mom could ask him about his day, he ran upstairs into his room and locked the door behind him. He was about to calm himself down, but when he turned around, he was met with a familiar-looking dragon sitting outside his closed window. It knocked again as Rex looked completely stunned.

DRAGON: Hey, it's me Akoi, remember?

REX: *Why are you here!?*

Akoi: To see if my mom got you on the team.

56

REX: *Well, she didn't. Now get out of my window!*

Akoi opened the window and slipped inside the room. She looked around at all the music sheets that were scattered across the floor. She picked one up before turning back into the form that Rex first met her in.

AKOI: You do music? That's so cool!

REX: Hey, put that down. It's private!

AKOI: *Oh, is that a guitar!*

REX: Hey! *Hey, get away from that!*

She picked up the guitar, playing around with the knobs a bit, to the absolute horror of Rex. He ripped the instrument from her hands, petting it a bit, before giving Akoi as mean of a look as he could muster.

AKOI: See, I knew I was right. You're special like me. I can
    tell it!

REX: What are you on about? You and your mom are crazy.

Akoi shrugged him off as she got closer to him in a well-meaning, friendly, but overall invasive manner.

AKOI: Come on, I know there's something special about you.

REX: Well, there isn't, and I don't want anything to do with
    this stuff.

He gripped his guitar tightly as he said the last line. Akoi started to get confused at his outburst.

AKOI: Why are you so mean all the time? Is it because you're
    hungry? Cause my mom says I get like this when I'm
    hungry.

REX: Just go away.

AKOI: Fine, I'll see you later, Mr. Grumpy Face.

She turned back into the dragon like before, then she looked out the window a bit. Before she left, she turned around to Rex one last time. Her voice shifting from her cheeky voice to a more serious tone.

Akoi: You'll see what I mean. I know it. You'll come around
    eventually.

She left in a hurry, leaving Rex alone in his room.

Eventually, his brother came back home, and they all had dinner. This brings us back to him holding the same guitar in his hands and finally walking over to his brother's room in the middle of the night with him fast asleep within.

Rex: Gavin, wake up. I need help.

The older brother didn't wake up, leaving the younger to be alone just as before. He wondered for a second.

Rex: What does he do anyway that would need him to
    sleep this much?

He sighed a bit as he sat down right on the floor next to the bed.

Rex: I'll just ask anyway. Well, there are these two people
    that want me to do something I don't want to do. I can't
    say no to them, and one of them is really cute. What
    should I do?

Even if it was to the snores of his brother, it was nice to get it all off his chest. To himself, he hoped that whatever happens next will be just as easy as telling someone else that.

11

GAVIN: *Where am I?*

I felt so heavy as I found myself in an almost pitch-black area. There were chains wrapping around the place several times. I pulled myself off the floor as I realized that there was a chain wrapped around my neck. I tried to pull it off, but the second I touched it, it felt like my throat was burning. While panting, I realized there was another one on my leg. I stopped messing with the chains as I looked around more and just saw more and more chains around the walls. As scary as it was, there was a strange comfort to them, almost like they were meant to be here. I closed my eyes as I smelled a strong scent of flowers, which calmed my nerves so much. I felt something shake me a bit, and I woke back up in my bed. It was my dad gently shaking me awake.

DAD: Gavin, wake up.

GAVIN: I-I'm up. Thank you, Dad.

My father patted my back with a smile before giving me a stern frown. I knew what words were coming next as I mentally prepared myself.

DAD: You're not slick, young man. We know that you've been sneaking out late at night. Now all that me and your mother ask is that you treat her nice and be responsible.

GAVIN: Yes, si—*a girl?!* I'm not—

I thought about it in a split second. If I just played along, then I wouldn't need to tell my parents what I'm really doing late at night. I just nodded along with him as he got off my bed, stepping on the books I had scattered on the floor.

DAD: Oh, and clean this room up when you get the chance, please.

GAVIN: Yes, sir. It will be spotless when you get home, promise!

My room wasn't that bad. Some dirty clothes here, and some food wrappers there, but it was all out of the way. Then again, most of it was from before I had my *night walks.* I let out a long yawn as I started my usual routine. Before I knew it, Rex and I were already hopping off the train, walking past the same electronic store, and a TV inside was airing the news. It didn't say anything interesting other than a new exhibit being added to the museum elsewhere. Rex walked ahead of me as I watched a bit more. Then the scent of flowers drew my attention elsewhere. The smell was sweet. I could almost taste the sap right on my tongue, and yet something about the scent made my heart start to race a bit. I turned to my side, to be met with a shy, meek girl that looked about my age. She was vaguely staring off into the distance. For a moment, she just stood still before she turned her head, almost robotically, and stared at me. I was a bit confused at the interaction as the once bustling noises of the city suddenly turned to pure silence.

GIRL: …

GAVIN: Can I help you?

GIRL: Kit, you're back.

GAVIN: What?

I blinked as she disappeared from my sight. I looked around frantically. It creeped me out to no end. Who was that? What did she mean by "You're back"?

REX: Gavin! *We're gonna be late. Let's go already!*

GAVIN: S-sorry, Rex, but did you see that girl?

REX: What girl? Come on, let's go already.

GAVIN: Blue, you saw that girl, right?

BLUE: You were just standing still for a while with a very
pale expression. You continue to surprise and scare me.

I shook it off as I caught up to Rex, then we split ways to our separate schools. When I entered my classroom, I saw a few people talking about a field trip that we had planned today. I had completely forgotten about it due to all the events from the previous days. I reached into my backpack looking for the paper. Call it luck but I found it completely signed by my mother. I gave a sigh of relief as Molly nudged me on the back.

MOLLY: So, dude, you ready to go? I mean, energy plants are
boring, but that means I'll miss that math test.

She showed me her paper. The signature was forged beyond a shadow of a doubt.

GAVIN: You forged this?

MOLLY: Yeah, why? My grandmother wouldn't ever willingly
make me miss a test, so I forged it. Wasn't that hard.
Plus it's not like I can ask my parents to sign it.

GAVIN: Wow, how rebellious for the future sewing doctor.
Please don't tell me you also plan to forge your medical
licenses too?

She smacked me hard in the face for the joke, then she went to sit back at her seat in a mini huff. I let out a small chuckle as I did the same, waiting for this trip to start. My mind started to think about that weird dream from last night. What did those chains mean, and why did—

TEACHER: All right, class, the bus is here. Papers or you're
not going. Come on, let's go.

I lost my train of thought and got up with the rest of the class to handle everything else. The teacher grabbed everyone who was going on the trip and pooled us all into the tiniest of buses. I got to sit in a seat alone 'cause Molly was in a different bus, so I just used this as an opportunity to get some more sleep.

After several minutes of boring travel, we arrived at our destination, and there was one thing I noticed right away.

GAVIN: You know, for an energy company, it looks very well guarded.

BLUE: I don't like this place. It seems evil.

It looked like any other building, but the vibe it gave me was off. It's hard to really explain in words. I just didn't want to be here. It might have been the fact that my dad works for the rival company, so I see this as something to be fearful of, but I even noticed that Blue wasn't with me. It bothered me a bit, but I took it all in stride as the small tour started. The trip itself was like any other field trip as the tour guide met us at the entrance and showed us around the company and explained how the energy works, how it's regulated, and everything else. Yet there was one thing he left out that I wanted to ask. Since my dad also works for one, I already knew, but the fact they left it out was strange. Wouldn't it be the first thing any tour would want to lay out?

GAVIN: So where does this energy come from? Like I don't see any solar panels or wind blades anywhere.

The tour guide stopped for a moment. It was kinda creepy how long they stopped until they finally gave the answer. If they didn't know the answer, they could've just said so.

TOUR GUIDE: Company secret. Anyway, it's time for a quick lunch break. Rest all those brains of yours.

We were moved to a lunch area, and we saw other workers eating their lunch as they were passing out our lunch. The free lunch they gave us was just some poorly made sandwiches. I could honestly make a better one with half the ingredients they used here. There was a strange feeling again as I looked around the room at some of the people eating. There was this group of three that were talking about something I wanted to listen to.

MAN A: Ugh, I know it's free, but these sandwiches suck ass. Turkey would've been way be— wait a sec, you guys feel that?

MAN B: Kinda feels like a shadow is close by. *Focus up.*

One of them that didn't speak at all yet looked over at my direction as I went back to eating my horrid sandwich. I tried to ignore it, but the more that person loomed over in my direction, the more I started to wish I had an escape. It was kinda like that fire guy from earlier staring me down. I guess the tour guide could read minds because while forcing the sandwich down, trying to keep myself in check, he then angrily glared toward me.

TOUR GUIDE: Hey, kid, what do you have over here?

I looked around to see what could be troubling him as I pointed to myself, confused. It really did help me forget about the feeling of that guy staring at me at least.

GAVIN: The sandwich you gave me?

The tour guide got closer to my face as he angrily pointed to my backpack lying at my side.

TOUR GUIDE: According to Relico rules, you are not
    permitted to have a personal carry-on if you are a visitor,
    and if you do so, it should be left at the front gate.

The guide tried to rip my backpack from me with me fighting back to take it back. Several other students also had theirs, so this was definitely targeted at me.

GAVIN: If this is about the energy question, I was just
    curious. Sorry, sir.

The guide then slapped me hard in the face, ripping the bag out of my hand. Molly was the only one to notice as I rubbed my cheek that was slapped.

TOUR GUIDE: This backpack shall be confiscated and
    returned to you in four to six days.

GAVIN: H-hey! Give that back. Why even that long?

TOUR GUIDE: After recent events, I must follow proper
    procedures to prevent further damages

GAVIN: I guess that's not so bad. What is this procedure
    like then anyway?

TOUR GUILD: Incineration and whatever's left you can recover. Now onto the last stretch of the tour!

GAVIN: Wait what?!

Before I could even argue back, the group began to move on without even saying another word. Molly walked over to me and slightly pulled me over before looking at the tour guide angrily.

MOLLY: Did that guy just punk you? What's his problem?!

GAVIN: He hated that I was curious, but my backpack...

MOLLY: It's just a backpack. I'm more angry at that guy being a dickwad. I should show him a piece of my mi—

I stopped her, placing a hand on her shoulder, shaking my head while mouthing out a single no. She rolled her eyes a bit as she finally calmed down with a disappointing sigh.

MOLLY: That's just so bullshit! Aren't you even a little bit mad?!

GAVIN: A bit, but I need my backpack back. There's something really important inside them.

MOLLY: What? Smart nerd stuff like books? It can't be that important—unless it is.

GAVIN: Well, you could say it's world-ending if I don't. It's fine, I'll get it back somehow.

My heart started to race as I remembered that the shards were deep inside that bag. Molly and I were stuck in the back of the group, and she started rambling, saying that we should double team the guide to get the bag back, but I shot each of her idea down, saying that I had a plan to get it back. The plan in question was to wait till night and just grab it as a fox. A quick in and out without hurting everyone. Hey, what's the worst that could happen, right?

CHAPTER

12

Now, while Gavin is interested in his backpack, his brother was less ecstatic. With the looming threat that he would have to be with his previous kidnappers again, he saw school, which once was a place of boredom, to be the only place where he didn't need to see the witch Telum or the dragon surprise of Akoi. After the two brothers split their usual ways, Rex started to walk slower till he remembered something great today.

REX: Oh yeah, we have a sub today! *That means I can do whatever I want in class! Yeees!*

With the thought of the two out of his mind, Rex ran right into his school and directly into his classroom, excited for what he could get away with. He was so excited, in fact, that he never realized the familiar girl sitting right next to him.

AKOI: Hi, Rex.

REX: *Yo, what's u—*

He looked back to see the warm smile of Akoi, who was giving a small wave.

REX: *What are you doing here?*

AKOI: I don't know. Mom told me to follow you today.

REX: *Of course, she did.*

AKOI: After this school thing, she said we're going to do something fun together.

REX: *Fun, right.* This day can't get any worse.

AKOI: Ugh, you're no fun. *Borrrrring.*

With some luck, the sub that the two got for the day was extremely laid-back, allowing the troublemakers in the class to mess around with whatever they wanted. All of them did, save Rex, who had to keep an eye out for Akoi, who was asking every students the strangest questions. It got to the point that he was hovering over her like a hawk, and just like kids do, they all started to call them a couple, to the horror of Rex and the confusion of Akoi.

Eventually, the day ended, and all Rex wanted to do was go home and scream into his pillow, but the dragon girl had other plans.

AKOI: Hey, Rex, where are you going?

REX: Home. Where you should be going too.

AKOI: But remember, we're going to do something fun together when we get home.

Rex: Yeah, you and your mom. Not me.

Akoi: No, she wanted you there too. It'll be fun, promise!

She grabbed his hand and started dragging him back to her home happily like a game. Rex tried to fight back, but her grip was like a bear trap, not letting him go. Once more, he was kidnapped, by an actual kid this time.

REX: *Help!* Somebody help me!

Instead of doing something, adults that saw the two of them just thought we were a cute couple or a pair of annoying kids. Rex eventually quieted down, and he walked with Akoi back to the same house he ran from so long ago.

AKOI: Mom, I'm back with the guy.

REX: I'm not just some guy. We're probably the same age.

AKOI: You're twelve?

REX: Eleven.

AKOI: Heh, *I'm older.*

TELUM: Ah, welcome back you two. You guys ready 'cause we're going on a little field trip. Don't worry, Rex, I already told this to your parents you'll be fine with us.

AKOI: Oooooh, where? Where? Where?

REX: I just want to go home.

TELUM: Sorry to disappoint you, Akoi, but we have to get Rex up to speed on the main problem.

AKOI: Aw, man, we're going there again?

REX: Going where again?

Akoi and Telum looked at each other and then back at Rex.

TELUM: I told you before that me and Akoi caused the entire shadow mess. Now I'm going to show you where it all started. There was something that I hid and hope it is still over there.

The two of them started to walk into a car located in a garage. Akoi motioned Rex to hop into his grumpy and unwilling self.

REX: So where are we actually going?

TELUM: You'll see.

Within a few minutes of driving, they had already driven outside of the city limit, heading into a vast wasteland of a desert. The more they drove, the more the city lights started to fade into the sunset of the desert. The ride was silent for the most part till Telum finally said, "We're here." Rex looked outside of the car to see the only thing left was a gigantic crater that looked like an explosion took place.

REX: *Woah, a big hole in the ground. What fun.*

TELUM: Just follow us.

AKOI: *If you're not scared, that is.*

Akoi and Telum slid down first, leaving Rex to follow behind. Telum slid down with grace; Akoi slid down on her back as if she was going down a slide; and Rex tumbled down after tripping, picking up a small dust cloud as he continued to tumble. Then they all finally got to the center and made sure Rex was okay. There was a small metal hatch. Telum opened it and motioned the others to follow her inside as she hopped down.

Rex: You know, I'll just wait—

Akoi grabbed his hand as they both jumped into the hatch into the darkness.

Rex: Aaaaaaahhhhh…

Telum: You can stop screaming now.

Rex: Aaaaahhh, huh?

Rex slowly opened his eyes to the revelation that he was alive, being held like a baby in Akoi's arms. He quickly pushed her off in an attempt to not look helpless in front of her.

Akoi: You know that it was only a small drop, right? You'd
    been fine even if you landed face first.

Rex: *Yeah, I knew that.*

Akoi just laughed and called Rex a wimp before he could even get back up. When things finally calmed down, Telum instructed the kids to follow her a bit further to a metal door. When they got inside, it was a complete mess everywhere. Broken computers and cracked tubes were dangling in a wild manner. Several chairs and tables were covered in burns and slash marks. Any lights that were left alone were flickering on and off, struggling to stay alight. Telum and Akoi just walked around the carnage like they knew the place's layout already, leaving Rex slowly being left behind to observe everything. It also didn't help that the young boy was terrified walking around the place, and every step he took made his heart race. Telum constantly had to stop to check up on him, sighing hard, walking back to pick him up by the shoulder. Eventually, they hit a wide open room that was worse than the others. Its walls scorched pitch black from what Rex thought was a fire.

Rex: What is this place?

Akoi: Well, it's kinda like—

Telum put a small hand on Akoi's head to make her silent as she understood.

TELUM: So about six, maybe seven, months ago...*god, has it really been that long already?*

REX: What?

TELUM: Ugh, nothing. A while ago, me and a team were sent here to check out this location due to some strange activities in the area. We didn't find anything, and most of the team got lax. Well, except one of us. He found this place, and I'm not even sure what the hell he really found. By the time I got to him, we both—

Her voice stopped, then she looked down a bit. Akoi was looking at her mother, confused, before she accidentally sneezed to bring Telum back up to speed.

TELUM: Anyway, that guy left me three things I need to keep safe. First, this hard drive with a lot of information that I'll tell you guys both later. Second, he told me to grab someone, and that person was—

AKOI: *Rex!*

REX: Wait, me?

TELUM: No, it was...*forget it.* The important thing is the last thing—that crystal right over there.

She walked over to a heap of rubble and started to move some away, to show a bright white shard underneath.

TELUM: I would've taken this with me when I was escaping the first time, but something else had my attention at the time. Glad those asses turned tail and left this place alone. Rex, get over here.

Rex stood still, rubbing the back of his hand a bit, till Akoi pushed him closer to Telum.

TELUM: Okay, so these crystals are very special. When you hold one, they can grant someone with strange powers,

or something like that. Both Akoi and I got one, and
now this one is yours.

She shoved the crystal into his hands as he looked at it confused.

Rex: So I can get cool mind powers like you or become a
cool dragon like Akoi?

Telum: We'll see. After you get them, we'll start training
tomorrow after you're done with school.

Rex: What kind of training?

Telum didn't say anything after that, just deciding to slightly hit Rex
on the head as he gripped the crystal over his head in a mild amount
of pain. Before he could yell back, he noticed that he was floating in
a dark area surrounded by stars. He was just looking around at all the
stars when he felt something tap his shoulder.

Akoi: Rex, you okay?

He blinked a few times as he realized the crystal was gone from his
hands. He didn't feel any different as he tapped his chest a bit.

Telum: How do you feel?

Rex: Um, I feel normal? Maybe it didn't work—

He raised his arms behind his head, and he noticed four small rings
surrounding his arms like halos, glowing a strange shade of blue. There
were two rings that were floating around each arm. He swung his arms
around. Akoi was nothing but amazed.

Akoi: Woah! So, so *cooooool*!

Rex: *How do I turn them off?!*

Telum: We need to figure out how they work first. Just
calm down—

Rex: *Get it off, get it off, get it off, get it off!*

In a rightful panic, he accidentally hit Akoi, and she was sent
tumbling over a bit, to the fear of both Rex and Telum.

Rex: Oh shit!

Telum: *Akoi, are you okay?*

She came bouncing up as if nothing happened, completely unfazed.

Akoi: Yep, yep.

Telum sighed in relief before returning to helping Rex with his rings.

Telum: Okay, Rex I need you to breathe in and out calmly.

Rex: *I am calm!*

Telum: Then stop yelling.

Akoi: It's easy. See.

She turned into her dragon form and took a deep breath and turned back.

Akoi: Now you try.

Rex looked at the two a bit before he closed his eyes, taking a deep breath, as the rings slowly faded away.

Rex: Are they gone?

Telum: Good job. Now back to the car. It is getting too late for kids like you, right?

Telum began to head back, leaving the two kids alone a bit. Akoi gave a mini thumbs-up, chuckling a bit as she ran after Telum. Rex looked at his hands a bit, then one thought came through his mind. He was so awesome. He ran after the two as they all got back in the car and drove back to the city. They dropped Rex off at his house, with Akoi hanging out the car window a bit, then they drove off.

Akoi: Bye, Rex. See you tomorrow.

He sheepishly waved, then he walked inside to see his brother and mother waiting for him.

Gavin: Sup, dude. Welcome back.

Mom: So how was the tutoring session?

Rex: Very...*informative*, I guess.

Mom: That's good to hear.

CHAPTER

13

GAVIN: All right, midnight. Time to go.

Before I left home, I stretched one last time as I mentally made a plan on what I needed to get done. From the tour earlier, I did learn that the boiler room leads directly into the center of the facility into the lower floors. All I have to do is hop down one and work my way up to get my backpack. It's not the best plan, but it's better than just walking right into the front door and just asking for it. Then again, I did learn how to break locks 'cause I got locked out the house one too many times. Maybe I'm more of a bad guy than I think.

BLUE: Hey, Gavin, you should go now. The sooner the better.

GAVIN: I know, I'm just bracing myself.

BLUE: Smart. Good luck. I still don't like that place. I'll watch from afar. Don't be long.

I hopped out the window, as I turned into my kitsune form, making my way to the company. It would just be a quick in-and-out situation. This will be easier than making a better sandwich than the school trip.

—ᴍ—

MAX: Man, nothing has been happening. It's been soooooooo boring around here.

ZACK: Hey, we've been turning in criminals by the handful. It's actually a blessing that those things haven't shown their ugly-ass mugs.

MAX: I guess, but don't you wish something would just happen?

RH just shrugged as they looked over to Zack, who was still angry, sitting with his shoes over the table.

MAX: Come on, why doesn't the fight just come to us then?

ZACK: 'Cause they know their place, *unlike someone else I know.*

MAX: *Oh yeah, Mr. High and Mighty over here.*

Zack gritted his teeth a bit, then the room had a long period of silence.

ZACK: So is that everything we need to talk about tonight?

MAX: I guess so. Welp, it's time for me to hit the hay.

ZACK: I guess so too. All those tests and training stuff. They're helpful, but they take so damn long to finish.

The two began to leave the room as RH watched the group leave. Max left the room first, but Zack stayed back, inching sheepishly to RH.

ZACK: Hey, RH, you gonna be okay?

RH shot him a thumbs-up in response with a smile.

ZACK: Okay then. Don't stay up too late with whatever. Rest is important.

RH stayed still for a moment with her thoughts. It had only been a few days, but she had grown a liking to this small group. The thing that made her the most happy was the fact that Zack was the only person to know about her secret. After all, as long as no one asks, she looks very convincing as a guy. She left the room with a long stretch, then she watched the security cameras a bit. Strangely, there never seems to be a night guard to do this, so for the past few nights, when she doesn't have to go on patrol, she does this for a few hours. Max's words rang through her mind as she shook it off.

RH: *Bring the fight to us. I hope not.*

—⚡—

GAVIN: Okay. That took way too long to get here.

I look at the outside of the large facility from the closest building to it. Getting here with the trains and buses was the easy part, now comes the hard part. I started to feel the same cold aura from before as I started to make my way to the roof of the facility.

GAVIN: All right, plan to infiltrate the energy plant is a go.

I looked around for the best way in, so I climbed to the tallest pipe and looked down into the deep darkness below. Bits of the steam stuck to my fur, and I whipped the water droplets off to the side

GAVIN: Okay then, let's see if I'm also fireproof.

I hopped down the pipe, and hot steam blasted me in the face as I slid on the side of the burning metal.

GAVIN: Hot, hot, *hot, hot, hot,* hot. *Haaaaaaaaaahaaaa!*

I only had to endure it for a few seconds before I entered the boiler area. I landed right on a railing over a boiling pot of scalding water. I tried to calm down a bit before I started my exploration, but it felt like my entire lower body was on fire, and I was struggling to keep my voice down.

GAVIN: Ha, *ha-ha!* Okay. Cooling down now. Way too hot.
   Okay, now where do they hold those stolen items?

I had to move fast if I didn't want to get caught or, worse, seen. Then, again, during that tour, I did see how the security room was almost bare. I'll be fine.

—⚡—

Yet little did our fox friend know, today was not one of those days.

RH: Ugh, it's the same old thing as last time. That one guard walking for five minutes on that camera to this camera, the other one walks from here to there, that fox runs from that door to...*wait a sec.* Isn't that?! Is that a fox? What is it doing here? I need to get the guys.

RH got up from the room and started to hurry toward Max and Zack's rooms, cursing over and over in her head at what Max said earlier.

—⁕—

GAVIN: Ugh, not this room...not this one either. Jeez, where do they keep their stolen stuff? It's just more rooms of pipes and hallways. I swear this entire place is a maze out of a video game.

I ran from room to room, finding weird things. A generator, another boiler room, an area that looked like a small lab. It was getting annoying looking at the random rooms. I ran higher and higher into the facility, checking as many rooms as I could. The only thing on my mind was who designed this place—that was, till I saw a room labelled "Authorized Personnel Only."

GAVIN: This looks interesting. Wonder what could be behind this giant metal door? Perhaps a bag that belongs to me.

The door had a passcode pad on the side, but I learned how to reset one of them. I still remember my dad yelling at me to hurry up and reset it after I locked him in his own office. You just had to hit a certain spot, and just like that, the new code can be set to anything I want.

GAVIN: 0000, easy as pie. *Thanks, Dad.*

I walked inside with no trouble at all. But instead of finding a backpack, I found more test tubes that were filled with the same shards I've been collecting.

GAVIN: What in the—? Why are these here?

I know I should've moved on to a different room, but this place was so weird. There was a huge computer screen with what seemed to be life vitals for three people. I guess this was the hero's medical bay. But what really caught my attention were the shards I was collecting that was on the table. We're these guys collecting them too? It didn't matter in my eyes what they were going with; I just moved on to the next thing in the room that was labeled *"Dark Force."* It was a small black thing just floating in a large tube. I stared at it a bit, and I swore I saw a yellow eye stare right dead at me for a second. I ended up punching the glass hard in response, cracking it to the point of almost breaking through it.

GAVIN: What the hell was that? *Fuck, calm down, idiot. Gotta keep moving.*

I was about to leave the room when the door locked behind me, leaving me stuck inside. I looked around the room to find another way out, then I saw a vent above the experiment tube that I was just looking at. I slipped in, grabbing all of the shards from the table and tubes, and made my escape through the vents. I guess I knocked something else in the room while leaving 'cause I heard a glass break. Well, I hope so anyway. It didn't seem important, so I focused on going to the next room over to find my backpack.

GAVIN: Ugh, it's so gross in here. Why do the movies make this seem so easy?

Now the vents were really filthy and grimy, and apparently, it can't support more than six pounds of weight as I fell through the ceiling. Call me unlucky 'cause I landed right next to someone.

GAVIN: Oh, I'm sorry. I'm sor—

I think they were just as surprised as me when we bumped into each other 'cause we both hopped backward onto a fight stance. I realized it was another member of those heroes. *He* looked at me funny as I tried to make any kind of small talk.

GAVIN: Hi, there. So what's your power? We got fire, lightning, and what are you? Wind? Water? Also, that's a very nice mask, looks very well made.

The person just stood there, not saying a thing. I couldn't see their face well with their mask and hat covering it so well, but their stance told me that I would probably get my butt kicked if they fought me.

GAVIN: Uh, you okay? The other two were *slightly* more talkative than this.

Again, silence. It was really starting to creep me out. They didn't even scoff at me or make a heavy sigh. It was like I was standing next to a brick wall.

GAVIN: *Okay*, I'll just take your silence as a warning and—

I booked it as fast as I could. If that guy saw me, then the other two might not be far behind. I was not in the mood to try and fight all three at once, especially on their home turf.

—✠—

RH was just confused that the fox, the thing that her teammates were struggling to defeat, was just running away from her. Also did it just complement her? It confused her for a second, but it didn't change the fact that she had to be the one to take him down. She realized that if it was as strange as it was, then it would leave the same way it came. In the moment, she debated on rushing to where the other two heroes were resting, but by then her legs were already halfway down a hall. A shortcut she knew that led straight to where the fox would be headed.

—✠—

GAVIN: *Nope, nope, nope, nope, nope!*

I started running past so many rooms, only stopping when I finally found it. A room label *"Contraband."* As I looked inside, I found my backpack, thankfully completely untouched from hours earlier.

GAVIN: Hey, my backpack! Took long enough to find this.
    Okay, now it's time to get the flip out of here.

I started running back down the facility, trying my best not to—oh great. The guy was waiting for me right next to the boiler room. Before I could even say anything, *he* shot a bullet of ice directly to my legs.

GAVIN: Woah, woah, woah. Chill, chill! Wait, *not like tha*—

The assault of ice didn't stop. I tried blocking as much ice as I could, using my tails to buy some time to think of a plan, but they just kept coming over and over like bullets. Eventually, they stopped, and my arms and tails stung in pain from the ice barrage.

GAVIN: You done? I really don't want to fight tonight and
wanna go home. Can we forget we met and just pretend
I was a bump in the night?

Apparently not, because *he* made a hammer out of pure ice and tried
to smash me over and over again. They were swinging like a master
'cause I was barely dodging the swings till one swing hit me dead in
the arm, launching me away into the boiler room. I was knocked all
the way into the edge of the railing. The boiler was right below, and the
guy followed.

GAVIN: *Okay…I just wanted…this backpack…and to get out of*
here. But if I have to go through you, then so be it. I didn't
want to be the bad person here.

The gloves were off now. I actually started to fight back. It wasn't
doing much 'cause we were both just dodging everything we both did.
That was when I came up with a great plan. I kept walking backward
closer to the boiler opening, and when *he* swung, I grabbed on to *his* leg
with my tail and made them almost fall into the boiling water, dangling
on the edge with one arm.

GAVIN: And that is how we do it. *Yeah!* Wait, oh no, that
was a bit too far, uh.

Before I left however, I did toss down a few strong wires next to
them to help pull them out. If anything, this should get me some nice
points hopefully. I hopped back up the walls, doing my best to not try
and burn myself on the way up. As I left the facility, all I could say was
one thing.

GAVIN: Worth it!

—◊—

Following the slip up at the hands of the fox, she climbed back onto
the railing to be met with Eugene's eyes.

EUGENE: That performance was sloppy.

RH: Eugene? Oh great, here comes the backlashing.

RH finished climbing back up then fixed herself as Eugene sighed hard at the mess.

EUGENE: And how did he even get in here? You three were supposed to be ready at all times. This is disappointing on your part. What's even worse is that he broke into— *the backpack room. That room.*

RH did take note of Eugene's sudden shift of mannerism before she looked back up at the vent the fox left through. The fox walked right up the wall side without any effort at all. Eugene recomposed himself, and he and RH left the boiler room. RH looked back up at the wires the fox dropped her before he left. He didn't have to, but they did. Maybe they weren't as bad as the other two guys said? But what did they want in that backpack?

EUGENE: Starting tonight, security here will be heavily increased. Now go get yourself cleaned up. I have an important meeting to attend.

Eugene walked into a secure room and answered a call.

EUGENE: Yes. I know the fox broke into the lab. Yes, the experiment broke free. Wait, that's a good thing? I see. Okay then. I'll keep you posted on any new changes.

Eugene hung up his phone and sighed.

EUGENE: That damn fox again. Here of all times and places…I can't let it destroy our work. Not again.

GAVIN: I did it, I did it, I did it. *Yahoo!*

I didn't care how I did it, but I did it. I got my backpack back. I was just happy to make it home. I didn't even notice Dad was also getting back home. I hopped through the window just as my dad opened my bedroom door. Without a plan, I just threw my blanket over myself before he could see me still in my kitsune form.

DAD: What are you still doing up so late?

GAVIN: *Uh, h-homework?* Mostly reading about flowers again.

DAD: Okay then, just remember it's a school night. Tell your friend you're talking to I said hi.

Gavin: Okay, got it! T-they say hi back.

BLUE: Does he mean me?

GAVIN: Heh, heh, yeah, Blue.

My dad left, and I finally calmed down from all the excitement today.

GAVIN: After all that, now I definitely need a break, and a long one at that.

I took a shower and went to a well-deserved sleep feeling amazing.

CHAPTER

14

The next day was weird between Rex and me. The two of us both woke up early and well rested. It was a first that I didn't have to wake him up early. It's like something changed in him, and it kinda creeped me out. Now that I think about it, anything not normal now sets off warning lights in my head. I just need to calm my nerves.

GAVIN: Morning, sleepyhead.

REX: Morning.

GAVIN: So what was your tutor thingy about yesterday?

REX: Why do you care?

GAVIN: Still as grumpy as usual, least you haven't changed.

We both made breakfast for ourselves, then we left for school together. Our usual walk was cut short as we passed the usual electronic store. Neither of us ever buy anything, but it is fun to look at all the TVs.

REX: Hey, why are people crowding over there?

He pointed over to a live reporter and their crew setting up right in the middle of the street. I wanted to say it was unlucky that they were blocking our path, but it was pretty rare to see how much stuff it takes for them to set up.

GAVIN: We got time. Let's see what this is about.

A few more people started to watch as the reporter began to speak.

NEWS REPORTER: This just in, the vigilante known to some as *The Fox* now has a bounty over their heads for breaking into Relico Inc. and possibly putting many people in harm's way. Any information regarding the whereabouts of the vigilante should be taken to the police. In other news, the Relico Saviors, as they call themselves, have started to make a name for themselves, furthermore...

PERSON A: I knew it. Never liked the bastard anyway.

PERSON B: Guess you can never judge a book by its cover. Too bad really.

CHILD A: But the fox guy saved people, Mom? Why is he the bad guy?

PERSON C: Not everyone is a good person, dear. Now let's go.

The crowd started to disperse, and we did the same. I thought Rex would say something about the report, but he stayed quiet too. Welp, at least, I know now that I can take a long, well-deserved break 'cause everyone is after me now.

Aside from that, I dropped Rex at his school with some girl waiting for him. It was the same girl from the train station from so long ago. Her eyes seemed to spark with an overzealous amount of joy when she saw Rex get closer.

AKOI: *Rex, what took you so long?*

REX: *Oh no.*

He ran behind me as the girl came closer to us.

AKOI: Come on, we have to go to your school place.

REX: I would gladly go. Without you!

I watched the two play a mini game of cat and mouse around me. It was cute.

GAVIN: So when are you going to tell Mom about your girlfriend?

REX: *Girlfriend?* Akoi isn't my girlfriend!

GAVIN: Akoi? Weird name.

I slightly bent down to give her a hand shake to her smile.

GAVIN: Nice to meet ya. Take good care of my brother, okay?

She looked at me before happily shaking my hand.

AKOI: I will.

Weirdly enough, the second I touched her hand, something felt different. I tried to let go as fast as I could, but I kept shaking her hand till we both were a bit creeped out by it. It kinda felt like we'd both met before. After that, I waved them goodbye as I had to get to my school now. I had a long day of doing schoolwork ahead of me after all.

REX: *Gavin, don't leave me!*

AKOI: So what are we doing today?

REX: *Noooooooo!*

I hurried up into class, enjoying being normal today. Though for some reason, I had this feeling I was being watched. I turned around a few times as the feeling didn't go away.

BLUE: You okay? You're starting to seem more paranoid than me lately.

GAVIN: It's just this weird feeling, you know? Not sure what, but it just is.

BLUE: Strange, I think I know what you mean however.

—✹—

Despite the pleas for help, Rex once again had to walk into class again with Akoi. It was at this time when the kids around Rex started to do what Gavin just did and accused the two of being boyfriend and girlfriend. It didn't help the rumors from spreading either when people asked Akoi about the two and said the words that sealed his fate. Rex was already labeled as a troublemaker with a bit of a reputation, and the rumors weren't helping him keep it.

AKOI: He is a boy, who is my friend, so yes, he's a boyfriend.

REX: *Akoi, please stop talking.*

AKOI: Why? I haven't said anything wrong, right?

The day for Rex seemed to just never end as the hours seemed to feel like years to Rex. To Akoi, who was happily and blissfully unaware of Rex's torment, sat beside him during the day's lessons. The day was filled with wonder and excitement. When the second the bell rang, Rex thought it was to go home, but to his dismay, it was just the bell for lunch. He dreaded the rest of the day as he grabbed his lunch, with Akoi following behind.

AKOI: Hey, this place is really fun! Why do you look so glum?

Rex let out a low grumble and sighed. Akoi pushed past him and smiled ear to ear.

AKOI: Really? You're still grumpy after everything? You need to lighten up a bi—

She stopped as she looked around, a bit concerned. Rex was confused at why as he felt a sudden jolt of energy that seemed to fill him up out of nowhere. Akoi was looking around the room looking like she just saw a ghost, lightly clenching her fist.

AKOI: (Whispering) *One of those shadows. A big one. It's in here. Look for it.*

REX: *Wait, for real?! You can't be serious.*

AKOI: *You feel it too, right?! Feel it out!*

REX: *How?!*

AKOI: *I don't know. Just feel it out.*

Rex started to look around the room full of kids in a frenzy when a sudden feeling of dread fell over him. He gave Akoi a small nod, and they both continued to look around the room wildly.

GIRL: *Help!*

Everyone in the room looked over to a lunch table where a girl was being lifted into the air by some invisible force.

GIRL: *Someone, help me, please!*

Everyone started to panic as the thing revealed itself. It was a giant chameleon-like beast. One that seemed to have its eyes ripped wide open to show nothing but rows of teeth. Rex felt just as helpless as everyone as the kid got closer to its jaws, till Akoi threw Rex's lunch tray right at it and it dropped the kid right on top of a table. The girl started to run as Rex threw Akoi's tray too, which turned the group of kids all stunned.

AKOI: *You okay?*

GIRL: *Y-yes.*

REX: *What's everyone standing around here for? Run!*

The second he said that, everyone started leaving the cafeteria in a panic. Akoi looked at Rex and gave him a wink. She was just about to transform, but Rex pulled her under the table, stopping her midway.

REX: You can't dragon out here, lizard breath.

AKOI: W-why not?

REX: 'Cause everyone will know it's you, dumb butt.

AKOI: Oh yeah, Mom said I couldn't do that with people watching. So what's the plan?

REX: *I don't know, Run?!*

They both continued to hide behind some tables, argue about what to do, while the chameleon was again trying to catch people. Luckily, their choice was made for them as a panicked teacher locked the two and several other students in the cafeteria with the beast.

REX: I hate people.

AKOI: Any other plans?

REX: You still can't dragon out.

AKOI: I know, but what other choice do we have?

As they were about to start arguing, the chameleon started to turn invisible and was hiding inside the room as it made a large footprint in the dropped food. That gave Rex a bright flash of inspiration.

REX: I got one plan.

AKOI: Well, what is it?

He grabbed some spilled food from the floor, throwing it randomly till it hit the beast dead on. The sauce of the food had made it visible.

REX: There, now we can stay away from it.

AKOI: Oh, I get it.

From there, it was just to avoid the giant invisible monster. Rex and Akoi both played around the beast, distracting it as best the they could and without using either of their powers. They seemed to be doing as well till Rex was grabbed by its tongue. Akoi was just about to break the promise to keep herself hidden when a large bolt of lightning crashed right through the wall, slicing the tongue off the beast and Rex fell to the floor, panting. Fulting ran over to the kids and started to sigh hard.

FULTING: Hey, you kids okay? We're so sorry we—

REX: *That was cool as hell.*

FULTING: Heh, thanks.

LIGHTER: RH, get the kids out of here. Fulting, you're
with me!

FULTING: *Right!*

A person ran in and started grabbing and guiding kids outside as Akoi and Rex ran with them. Akoi was looking very proud of herself as she showed Rex something.

AKOI: Hey, look! That thing dropped a lot of these things
when we were fighting it.

REX: *I almost died.*

AKOI: Ya, you'll get used to it! But really, look at these.

Her hands were filled with a myriad of shards, and she stuffed some into Rex's pocket.

Aĸoɪ: Mom said that we need these, so I want you to hold some, okay?

Rex: *All right. Sure, yeah.*

The kids were all left at the front of the school by the person with a red hat as they blitzed back inside to the other strange two. Several teachers and parents were already outside, apparently having heard of all the commotion. Rex's parents instantly hugged him tightly, even his brother was there for some reason.

Rex's Family: *Rex!*

Dad: *Are you hurt?*

Mom: *Are you feeling okay? My poor baby!*

Gavin: Rex, thank god, you're still okay.

Aĸoɪ: Don't worry, I kept him safe just like I promised.

Gavin: Oh, it's you again. You two really are inseparable.

Rex: I'm fine. You don't have to worry about me.

Dad: It's our job to worry about you.

The entire family embraced in a hug as Akoi just watched, slightly tilting her head. She looked back at the school.

Mom: Wait. Gavin, why are you here?

Gavin: My brother was in danger? Family over school. My friend is covering for me anyway—

Mom: *Get back to school right now!*

Gavin: *Yes, ma'am! I'll see everyone at home!*

He left as fast as he showed up. As he left, Telem ran up to the school with a sigh of relief as she saw Akoi next to Rex.

Telum: I see that you turned out okay.

Aĸoɪ: Hi, Mom!

Telum: Let's get you home. Today was not what I expected—

Aĸoɪ: Wait, I need to give you these.

She gave Telum some of the shards from earlier as Rex's parents started dragging him home.

AKOI: Later, Rex.

TELUM: These shards.

AKOI: Hm?

TELUM: I'm glad you grabbed these. We'll need them for something soon, you'll see.

CHAPTER

15

I slipped back into the classroom window as Molly looked at me angrily, her arms crossed. I sat back down in my seat to her kicking my leg angrily.

MOLLY: *You owe me. You know that rig—*

GAVIN: *Those shadow things just attacked my brother's school. Give me a break, please.*

MOLLY: *Never mind. Still owe me lunch later. Also, how did you get there and back so fast?*

GAVIN: *Uh, shortcuts.*

TEACHER: *What are you two blabbering on about?!*

GAVIN AND MOLLY: *Nothing, sir!*

The day went and gone, and I hopped back on the train back home. Molly was texting on my phone wildly about how sorry she was about her outburst. I did my best to calm her down. I started to think for a second, then I fully decided that I just took a long break. Besides, Molly did say we could go hang out over at the mall or something.

The second I got home, everyone was in the living room silently doing their own thing. Rex looked away from the TV.

REX: Hey, Gavin. School just got canceled for me, so I got a mini vacation!

DAD: You still have your tutor. Don't get too excited.

MOM: Especially with that failing grade of yours, but I can't be mad after today. Oh, Gavin, fend for yourself for dinner, okay?

GAVIN: Okay, I will.

I went upstairs to my room to put some things away, and Blue started to drag my attention to something.

BLUE: Hey, there's some shards close by. Really close.

GAVIN: I mean, yeah, there inside my bag, remember?

BLUE: I mean outside of your bag. They're in the room down the hall.

GAVIN: You mean my brother's room?

BLUE: Your sibling, yes. Grab them, it might be enough to—

GAVIN: All right got it, got it. Calm down already.

BLUE: I'm sorry, I just know that if my allies are trapped like me, then I want to save them as soon as I can.

GAVIN: They're your friends, and close ones from the sound of it. It's only fair you'd want to save them from whatever you were stuck in.

I walked back into Rex's room to get a quick lookaround. The same sheets of music paper were still scattered across the floor, with his guitar in the corner of his room. I did notice that the strings on them were starting to wear down a bit. Christmas is coming soon in a few months, maybe I'll get his gift early, and one for his *girlfriend* too. That aside, the shards were placed neatly right on top of his bed. A truthfully dumb thought crossed my mind that he might also have powers and was fighting those shadows too. It was a funny thought before I thought more about it. My brother fighting those beasts where I can't protect him. The thought scared me, and I quickly left his room and went back to my own room thinking about how he even got the shards in the first place.

—◊◊◊—

ZACK: Well, I think today went fine. Great work out there, guys.

Max started to sulk more into his seat as he looked at his hand, cleaning them hard.

MAX: Those shadows just keep coming out of nowhere. If we were slower, than those kids might have—

ZACK: Stop saying that. We did good, and that is all we have to do. No one was hurt, so what's the problem? Not to mention, we got a good deal of shards out of it.

Max stood up, getting closer to Zack adamantly, almost getting closer to his face.

MAX: They were kids with families. We have these powers, and we just barely made it. If I missed that shot, then I don't even want to think about it. *I wish I could've just teleported everyone out of there.*

ZACK: Well, you didn't. Maxie, you're always going on and on about stuff like that. In case you haven't gotten it through your thick skull, it's fine. We're all fine!

Max's eyes widened hard, and RH noticed what was just about to happen and got up right as Max balled up his fist.

MAX: I told you to never say my real name!

ZACK: Why not, Maxie?

MAX: *Why you fucking dick!*

The two tackled onto the floor, both landing hard punches over and almost punching RH with a few stray swings as she came to broke them up. The two were both blinded by rage as they struggled to reach each other through RH's grip.

ZACK: *Let me at 'em! I'll punch your fucking lights out!*

MAX: *Like you will, you prick!*

Quickly thinking, she froze both their legs to the floor, then she hit both of them in the head hard, snapping their attention to her.

MAX: *The hell was that for, man?!*

ZACK: *That's a girl, dipshit!*

MAX: *No! He's not a girl.* Wait, right?

RH gave a shallow nod as Max instantly calmed down and let out a long sigh.

MAX: I-I'm sorry. God, I'm so fucking sorry.

ZACK: Language. *The kids are watching, right?*

MAX: You—forget it. This is all stupid anyway.

ZACK: You're right, it is. Now hold still one sec.

Zack burned the ice off himself before helping Max. Eventually, the three sat back down and RH brought their attention to why this meeting was even called.

ZACK: What is it, RH?

She made a motion that looked like a fox as Max caught on.

MAX: Oh yeah. The fox broke in last night.

RH nodded her head, looking at the two, who both sulked back down.

ZACK: I'm sorry that we weren't there to help you out in the fight. Should've been awake.

MAX: I kinda see what you meant before, dude. The furball is kinda annoying. But I've been thinking. Maybe he isn't so bad, right? I mean, I've only seen the thing once, but he only seems to be doing good, right?

RH slightly nudged Zack as he sighed.

ZACK: Still, he could be the cause of all this. Look at it like this. The thing could be a third party that wants to use those shards for its own purpose, like a weapon or worse.

RH remembered when the fox threw down an extra rope to her after she fell. It didn't have to, but it showed kindness even to its attackers. Maybe Max had a small point.

MAX: All I'm saying is, maybe we should talk to it or something. Like as a group?

The room went cold for a while. Nobody had an answer to that question.

ZACK: When and if it happens, then we'll decided there. Is that something that can be accepted by everyone?

The two nodded.

ZACK: Okay then, I guess that's all for tonight.

The three got up, and they left the room. RH left first as Zack and Max stayed back for a second.

MAX: Hey, I'm sorry for earlier. I just got—

ZACK: No, it's my fault. I should be apologizing. You're right, hell to this all.

MAX: We're still cool, right?

ZACK: No, we're brothers-in-arms.

The two fist bumped before leaving the room. From afar, RH gave a slight smile in response to the boys.

CHAPTER

16

It had been a few days from the chameleon attack, and things have been going okay for the most part around town. Every day Rex would go over to his tutor and come home looking extremely tired, or rather, drained from the looks of it. I didn't bother him about it, mostly because he wouldn't tell me anyway. As for me, I've been resting, just heading to school and hanging out with Molly. She had been pulling me around after school to do some fun random stuff like going to the mall shopping for clothes, messing around at the library to help study for a test, or, today, where I was basically watching her work at that ice cream parlor. She said that I should apply here so we could work together, but I told her that I already have a job that pays decently well. I do have around $4,000 hidden in my room from all the criminals I took down. Think I'll use the cash for something later on.

MOLLY: Hey, Gavin, could you stop daydreaming and check this out?

GAVIN: Huh? What is it?

She was moving a small needle around some string. She was getting frustrated at it and passed it over to me. It had been a few minutes, and she was on break. I stop by the ice cream parlor every now and again to hang out and bother her while she worked.

MOLLY: I need to practice sewing, but I couldn't afford those expensive practice stuff, so I thought I'd just practice like this, but it sucks, right?

GAVIN: Hmmmm, yeah, it could be better. But it looks nice. Still, better than that awful handwriting of yours.

MOLLY: My handwriting is fine, unlike your confidence. You really have to stand up for yourself, you know that? Be strong and stuff!

GAVIN: I know, but I don't—

MOLLY: Nope, I'm not letting you. Tell you what? If I get this ribbon done, you have to start putting in the effort to stand up to people, okay?

GAVIN: Heh, sure I'll take that bet.

RUDY: *Molly, break's over! Get back to work!*

MOLLY: *Ugh,* say you wouldn't mind if I quit my job and applied for what you do, right?

GAVIN: Heh, sorry, but my job is *full* for the foreseeable future.

MOLLY: All right then, it's getting late. See ya at school tomorrow?

GAVIN: Right, see ya.

We both gave a friendly wave as I left the store, heading back home on the train, only to be met with the worried hovering of Blue. During this time, Blue has been extremely worried about me. I've been doing my best to calm him down, but if these shards don't turn into a compass soon, I'm not sure if he'll be okay. But on that note, I wonder if Rex is doing any better with his tutoring.

—⚏—

REX: I know we're getting close to what these rings do.

AKOI: I'm sure we'll get it.

The three were inside the house of Telum. Ever since the attack, Telum has been training the two for their future missions. After a lot of trials, and getting Rex to actually listen to her, Telum thought today would be a great day to figure out what Rex's rings could actually do, to the excitement of both kids.

TELUM: All right, kids. Ready to figure out what those rings can do?

REX AND AKOI: *Yeah!*

REX: Okay, let's see. Rings, flip on.

The blue rings appeared over his arms as Rex let out a little chuckle at how quick he was able to do it.

TELUM: You're getting better at that.

REX: Yeah, it's getting way easier after all the practice.

TELUM: Okay, let's see what we can check off the list this time.

With that, they went into what the rings could do. The day went on as they tested a myriad of ideas. Strength? Speed? Mobility? Flight? Nothing seemed to benefit them, and they all started to doubt what it could do.

AKOI: What if your ability is just to look cool? That would be nice, right?

REX: That's dumb. You have dragon powers, and Telum has physic powers. Mine has to be special somehow. It has too right? I can't be lame.

AKOI: Why does it matter to you? I thought you didn't like my *lizard breath*.

TELUM: You called her what?

REX: Wait, wait, wait.

TELUM: If you don't figure out that ability soon, I'll sling you home myself!

In a small panic of the threat, Rex started swaying his arms randomly, trying to calm down Telum as she moved closer to him. His flailing stopped when he shot a small beam from his hands, hitting the ceiling, to the shock of everyone.

AKOI: *Did you see that!* It was some blue arrow thing!

TELUM: Wait. Do that again.

REX: Oh, okay.

He tried it again and held his hands like he was holding a bow firing another beam of light. The girls didn't know it, but Rex noticed that a music note played any time he fired.

REX: I-I did it. *I did it! Yeaaaaaaaaaaaah!*

He ran over and hugged Akoi, to Telum's slight confused laughter.

REX AND AKOI: We did it, we did it, we did it. *Wahoo!*

TELUM: Nice job. Now we can get into the real stuff.

REX: The wha—?

TELUM: Now that we know what your power is, we need to
	work on its power, speed, disruptive power—

Telum started ranting on things that neither Rex nor Akoi could understand, but they both quickly got the impression that it would mean more work for all of them.

———∞———

I had come home after hanging out with Molly. Nothing much happened till I hopped off the train and saw the cat again. It had a single shard in its mouth. It dropped the shard as I got closer to it, to the absolute surprise of Blue and me. I picked up the shard as Blue looked at me. I already knew what he wanted to say, and I went back home to try on my idea.

GAVIN: Okay, shards, I think I have enough like last time.
	Turn into a compass. Please? Come on work with me!

I had been messing with the shards for a while but to no avail. I needed to keep my promise to that spirit. I clutched all the shards and whispered to them, almost praying.

GAVIN: Please. I need to find them.

BLUE: *Please.*

As if they had a will of their own, the shards started to shine like what happened last time.

GAVIN: Thank you.

BLUE: Woah, y-you did it. You really did it.

After the light show, I got my new crystal compass, though instead of the shining blue like last time, it was a burning crimson.

GAVIN: All right, I guess I know what I'm doing tonight.
 Don't worry, new spirit, I'll come save yah!

I waited for night to fall, and the compass seemed to be pointing into the city again. When all my family members fell asleep, I hopped out the window and transformed back into the kitsune form as I made my way into the city. It was way easier to stay out of sight with me using the rooftop of the building to traverse the night city. The compass led me to the city's museum, of all places. It was still closed for repairs, so thankfully, no one would be inside for the night. I found a window that was broken, and I hopped up to it on the roof. I was about to softly hop down, but the meowing from the same cat before scared me into tumbling into the floor.

GAVIN: *Ow, stupid cat.* Man, it's dark in here, and quiet.

The area was empty and almost ghostly to an extent. I could barely read or see any of the art pieces around me. I opened the compass as I walked around almost blindly in the dark, trying not to knock anything and accidentally set off an alarm. Thanks to the small glow from the compass, it gave a decent amount of light to get a good look at some of the things inside: old art, vintage books, etc. It wasn't till I was in the Egyptian section that things got interesting. The compass pointed directly at a wall that depicted a wall of gods. The thing that caught my attention was a statue depicting Anubis. Funny enough, I know a lot about the legends and history of this guy. He really reminds me of my father, with how strong and loyal he was, *ignoring his other bad qualities, of course.*

GAVIN: Oh great, another statue. Imagine if this one wanted
 to fight me too. Heh-heh.

I laughed a bit before I looked at the scale that the statue held. It was off, unbalanced with the lighter side having what looked like a spot made for the compass. Without any better plan, I placed the compass on, and the scales slowly tipped evenly. The second they balanced, sand and wind started to engulf my vision. I could do nothing against it. I immediately tried to shake off the sand in a wild panic, not wanting to get buried again till I got my vision back. I was starting to slide down a pit of sand, slowly falling deep below something. I struggled for a bit, and I managed to pull myself free from the sand flow. I looked behind me, and I realized I was locked in a room of halls again. Only this time the area resembled something that looked like the inside of a pyramid or a tomb of some kind.

GAVIN: It seems like I can't go back now. Okay, Gavin, let's go.

Just like the last time, I plunged into the dark corridors as that strange feeling of being watched went away. It wasn't much, but not having the dread of being watched helped me focus on what task I had ahead of me.

CHAPTER

17

MAX: So it's my day for patrolling, right?

ZACK: Yours was two days ago, remember? It's RH turn tonight.

RH perked up at that information. It had basically been forever since she had left, and she instantly started to put on her hat.

MAX: Hers? Isn't this her first time alone then?

ZACK: It's not my call. It's Eugene's.

RH looked excited at the news to go alone for her first time. This time she could show the boys how to really get the job done. She smiled at the two as she got up, getting ready to leave.

MAX: Hey, where are you going?

ZACK: We know this is your first time, and we're worried for you. I know that you have that special quirk but—

RH didn't even listen to the rest as she left for her first patrol. It had to be perfect. No, it will be perfect. She started to make her ways into the city as she realized what the boys meant. Unlike the others, she wasn't able to fly at will, at least not like this. Staying out of sight, RH started to patrol smaller areas around the city. It seemed way too quiet. She went around check areas that usual criminals would hang around and found no one. It was like someone or something made all of them scared or stayed hidden. Thankfully, or unthankfully, there were still a few running amok to keep her slightly busy. Overall, it was a quiet night until she got a call from Max from her flip phone.

RH: *How did they even find my num—?*

Max: Hey, RH, how are you doing?

There were sounds that she guessed were Zack pushing Max out the way as his voice began to overpower Max's.

Zack: Are you hurt? Are you feeling okay out there?

RH rolls her eyes as she really couldn't say anything about her safety for obvious reasons. She could hear the silent sound of stupidity from the other side of the phone as Zack's voice came back over.

Zack: Anyway, we're here to tell you about a possible disturbance close to you. Be safe.

Max: Also, if you can, you're closer to this old food place I used to visit, bring us back some—

RH quickly hung up on Max as she went to find the possible disturbance. While moving around, she lamented on what she learned about both her teammates based on what they have said around her and during their minor training sessions. Zack, or Lighter, was brash and rough on the edges; but when he's alone with her, he's very sweet and honest. He seemed quite hurt about a past event because anytime a person brings any kind of alcoholic beverage near him, he leaves the area angry. On the almost complete opposite, she has Maxie, or Fulting. He's extremely outgoing and very vulgar about wanting to do right. Though similarly, he always gets a minor panic if he's not somewhere early, apologizing almost to a point of almost begging for forgiveness, not to mention that he constantly brings up food to any conversation for some reason or another. Both men were strange, but anything would be better than what she left behind in her past. Eventually, she got close to the disturbance as she saw a whole bunch of people huddled in an alley.

Person A: What do you fellas say about that fox guy?

Person B: You mean that guy that's been taking those criminals out? I personally like the guy.

PERSON C: Remember those Relico whatever's going after 'em too. Any info on it will make us rich, right?

PERSON B: Duh, but first we gotta find it, right? What info do we have on it?

PERSON D: We have some small info so far. It's been spotted every other night patrolling the downtown area, stopping small criminals. It doesn't show up often, but when it does, it always stays from around midnight to 3:00 a.m., then leaves. The exception to this pattern is when those shadows appear. It's guaranteed that it shows up and deals with a lot of those things.

PERSON A: I'm sure any person with half a brain could figure that out. What do we have that could be actually worthwhile? Its name, identity, where it lives?

A fifth person comes running inside, panting wildly as RH and the rest of the group took notice to how tired and worn out they looked.

PERSON E: Guys, I-I found out where the fox is! *Right now!*

PERSON C: *Where!* Where did you see it?

PERSON E: The museum. It's in the museum. It fell inside, and I don't think it'll leave for a while.

That's all RH needed to hear. She wrote down the information and gave the other two a call. This time that fox wouldn't get away from them.

CHAPTER

18

GAVIN: This place is just like that underwater area, minus
the fishy and sea smell.

The halls that I was walking through were loose as the walls seemed
to be leaking sand onto the floor. The hot and scratchy air made this
walk almost unbearable. I'm glad that I did prepare myself for this by
drinking a bit of water before I left home. Eventually, I walked into a
wide open room filled to the brim with books. I guess it was some kind
of library for someone. The second I walked into the room, the path
behind me got sealed up by sand, locking me in the room. I looked
around to see if there was another hallway I could walk down, but to
no avail. It was just me and all these books.

GAVIN: Man I wish I had the time to read some of these
right now. Then again, if I'm stuck in here, maybe there's
a hint on what to do here.

Without anything else to do, I picked up one of the books and
opened it. It was written in a language I couldn't read, so I just put it
back. I wandered the library a bit more before a book caught my interest.
It mainly had to do with two things. One, it was the same crimson
red like the compass I used, and two, it was in English. The second I
grabbed the book, it opened up to a blank page and started writing by
itself. It wrote out, "At long last, someone has come. Though, I wish I
could speak to you in person."

GAVIN: So you must be one of the spirits I was asked to save. Blue will be happy after I get you out of here. *Soon as I find a way out of here.*

The book started scribbling again, this time saying, "You helped one of us before? That makes things easier. So you already know that you need to break the chains that are keeping us trapped here?"

GAVIN: Chains? The last time I just wandered around till stuff started to attack me. Speaking of, do you know how I can get out of here by any chance?

The book scribbles one last time: "This area is simple to get out of. Just break that light above yourself."

I looked up at the light above me as a lantern was sawing creepily above me, like the fire itself was alive, waiting to be set free.

GAVIN: That lantern? Okay then.

I hopped up and kicked the lantern down. As it broke on the floor, the fire instantly started jumping from bookshelf to bookshelf as if it was dancing. The smoke coming from the burning pages quickly started to fill the room, making the air get thinner with each passing second.

GAVIN: Holy…uh, Book Spirit, why did I have to do that!?

The book scribbled again, "Those embers will show the exit. You'll see."

The dancing flame started to grow larger as I was forced to move out of the way several times just to survive its short-lived dance of freedom. This reminded me of when I first got my powers. It was only a few weeks ago, but look at me now. I was getting lost in the past, forgetting that the smoke was rising closer to me. Then I saw that some were flying away out to a hidden air duct, showing a way out.

GAVIN: Oh, a hidden ceiling hole. I guess it's time to try out one of the new things I've been working on.

I hopped up and ran up the secret hole using what I had been practicing with Blue. To walk up the wall as if it was the regular ground. Originally, it was just a lesson in how to stand on water, but I did my best to use the same idea, and I quickly got the hang of it, to Blue's surprise. It was also surprising to me at how well I *mastered* this trick. I was running up the wall, chuckling to myself a little bit about how well this was going. Way better than when I escaped Relico and slipped my way up that vent. Any case, I was out of the burning room, running to the top of the hole, to reveal a wide open area. For a second, I thought I had gone outside the museum, but when I entered, it was almost midnight, not midday like it was now. I looked back at the hole I jumped from as that, too, got sealed up like last time.

GAVIN: Welp, I guess it's comforting that something around
    here is consistent.

The book started to shake again, getting my attention. This time it scribbled, "It approaches. Be careful and make decisive blows." Right as I finished reading, the ground started rumbling. I tried to find my footing as the rumblings got closer.

GAVIN: H-hey, thanks for the heads up! All right, let's get
    this thing out the way.

Finally, out of nowhere, a giant stinger came out the sand. It was a surprise and not a welcoming one. Just like last time, it was a giant version of an animal. This time being a scorpion.

GAVIN: All right, another day, another giant beast. I'm
    starting to think that I'd be a great fit for pest control.

This was a very risky place to fight. I don't really have much mobility in the sand, but I had to figure out some kind of plan as the huge buglike monster started attacking.

GAVIN: Hey there, can't we work something out? You know,
    like us not wanting to kill each other? No? Well then.

It had two giant pincers to deal with first and its giant stinger. It wasn't that much to juggle, but the thought of getting even a bit of poison on or near me made my plan to be way more defensive. It also didn't help that I hated looking at this thing. Okay, personal gripe, I hate anything that even resembles a spider. They just look so gross and have way too many eyes and legs, and the fact that these things are also practically blind is just stupid. It didn't matter anyway about what I thought because if I wanted to save that spirit, then I had to get through it. I took a deep breath and jumped right on top of it. Like I knew it would, it slammed its stinger, trying to hit me. I dodged it and just to quickly end this fight and to test out my own strength, I grabbed its stinger and started to take it for a spin. The scorpion was surprising light for its gargantuan size. However, just holding on to it made my skin crawl.

GAVIN: Gross, gross, gross, gross, gross, gross, gross.

I threw it high into the air, and without hesitation fired a fox fire, quickly vaporizing most of its body. The fight was over after that, as it tried to run away before falling over itself, fading away like how the shadows did. Defeating it caused a part of the sand to open up a sinkhole down into the dark depths below. With nothing else to do up here, I hopped down back into the pyramid-esque tomb. I opened the book to try and talk with the spirit. It was going to be a boring walk anyway considering with how boring and hot it was here.

GAVIN: Sorry you had to see that. I really should be more used to this stuff by now. Oh right, I've tried to ask Blue, but he can't seem to remember what happened to you all. If you can, I want to know more about everything. The shadows, you guys, and whatever happened to me. I know it's a lot but anything would really help right now.

The book didn't change in the slightest. I guess it either didn't have an answer for me, or it was writing out a very long answer. It didn't faze me now anyways, I just wanted to save this spirit and get out of this heat.

19

MAX: RH, hey you're back. Aw, no food?

ZACK: You're back early. Did you fin—

RH slammed a piece of paper in front of them with large text written on it: *Follow me. I know where the fox is! Let's go now!*

MAX: Wait, you know where it is?!

She nodded crazily as the two boys switched on their powers in a fit of excitement.

MAX: Finally, some real action! *You ready?!*

ZACK: This time I'll get the bastard for sure.

MAX: But didn't we all agree to—

ZACK: I know. That's why I have a plan. Let's move!

—⚂—

GAVIN: Man, it's getting hot as flip in here.

The hallway I was walking through just seemed to get warmer and warmer as I walked deeper to wherever I was going. I had taken off the sweater I have on whenever I turn into a kitsune and wrapped it around my waist to try and cool myself off, but it only helped for a bit. I felt like I was getting closer to where I needed to be, but I still felt like I was getting nowhere. That's when I finally felt the book start to shake again.

GAVIN: You answered my question, right? That took you a
minute. Let's see here.

The book read, "So you want to know about those shadows, as you
and many call them. Well, it all started in my time hundreds of years
ago. We were just living peacefully till a creature of absolute horrors
attacked our world. I remember four of us all standing together to
sealing away a calamity god in a crystal before parting ways. Past that
I don't remember much, except fighting several humans to protect
something. Then my attention was dragged away for one second, and
I was stuck. Something broke. I apologize for the wait and the lack of
information. My memory is not what it used to be."

GAVIN: Okay then. Thanks really.

That was kinda redundant. That gave a bit more to the backstory
of the spirits, but that didn't answer my questions about me. At least, I
know about this dark crystal thing.

GAVIN: So what do I do then? Is this calamity god thing
still out there? You fought it before right? It must've had
a weakness, right?

The book quickly scribbled something else. "If I knew how it was
resealed I would tell you. But from what I do remember, someone said
that the fight was hopeless."

GAVIN: Great, so we need a miracle then…This all seems
kinda pointless. If this calamity thing shows up, then—

I slapped myself immediately after saying that.

GAVIN: This heat is getting to me. I won't let it happen, duh.
I can stop it just like that scorpion. It's just like mom
said, win and don't hold your tricks.

I really gave myself a good pep talk 'cause I hit the same intimidating
door without noticing it again. The only difference this time was that I
was ready for the worse.

GAVIN: Okay, it's big, bad boss time. *Let's do this!*

I kicked open the door to see an empty room with only a casket
inside. It was way cooler in the room than the hallway, so I already felt
better. I took in the less warm air for a moment before the door shut

behind me. The second this happened, all the torches around the walls blew out except one, the one next to the casket on the other side of the room.

GAVIN: I guess it wants me to go there, huh?

The book shook one more time. It read, "Please stay alive and fight with all your power, for both our sakes."

GAVIN: Don't worry, I got this.

I walked up to the casket and slowly began to open it. The second I opened it, I jumped back in anticipation of an attack, but none came. I slowly looked into the open casket, expecting the worst, but all that I found was what looked like a deformed corpse. Inside was an all-black jackal with gold jewelry. It was kinda similar to how I looked, but ancient. Wait, isn't this how people depicted Anubis? I started looking over what I hoped was a corpse. It's eyes we're still closed, so that gave me hope.

GAVIN: Let's see, jacked figure? Check. Jackal-like appearance? Check. Gold jewelry and white clothing? Check. White eyes that can stare into my soul. Che—*oh shit.*

I panicked as the fucking protector of death just stood up from its tomb and looked dead at me. I struggled to even find the will to breath as he started to walk toward me.

GAVIN: UhhiAnubisgodlordofdeathuhwhatyadoinghere? (Uh, hi, Anubis, god…lord of the dead. Uh, what ya doing here?)

I quickly took as many steps back as I could and quickly opened the book without ever losing eye contact with Jackal.

GAVIN: What the hell? *How am I supposed to beat the person who literally judges souls for a living? Did you beat this guy?!*

All I got in response was the most helpful thing in the world. "Why would I need to beat—"

The last line was cut off as the book dispersed into sand, falling out of my hands before I could finish reading.

GAVIN: I'm starting to see why the calamity kicked your
guy's butt.

I didn't notice that I had lost track of my foe, with my eyes darting around the room in a frenzy to try and find him. I was trying not to lose it and stay as calm as possible when I heard something close to my ear.

ANUBIS: A kitsune? How rare.

I hopped as far away from him as I could get away with to the other side of the room, picking up a small cloud of sand as I halted my movements.

GAVIN: L-look. I was ready to fight a giant monster, not
death himself. C-can't we ju—

ANUBIS: You? Fight me? That's a surprise. Many have tried
kit, and none have succeeded. Do you really think you'll
be the first?

Okay so, what even, how do I even, and…you know what? Fuck it! Molly was right. I've been a coward. It's time for me to grit my teeth and fight like I mean it!

GAVIN: It's either I do nothing and die, or I try and die
either way. One will just be more self- fulfilling, I guess.
Bring it on!

I had nothing to lose and everything to gain. I took a defensive stance and got ready for the assault.

ANUBIS: Let's see how long you'll last this time.

He blitzed right for me as I just barely could dodge most of his hits. I was honestly too terrified to actually retaliate back, so I just kept dodging hits. His hits felt like I was being rammed into a large wall over and over. Any hit he did land felt like I would pass out easily. I guess this was a new feeling for the jackal god 'cause he got pissed fast, moving faster with his rapid assault on me.

ANUBIS: *Stop dodging and fight back!*

With that, he got a single good kick on my side, launching me across the room into the wall. I lay still for a solid minute before Anubis walked over to me, picking me up by the tails and slamming me into the ground and wall again. I finally got back up, trying desperately to think of a plan as I struggled to catch my breath, holding my chest side in pain. I thought of something on the spot as Anubis started to yawn in boredom.

GAVIN: Okay then, let's see if Blue was right.

With Blue, we focused on two types of training, one was with water walking and the other was about my aura. Blue said that if I wanted to, I could form my aura into most things like weapons, knowing that I thought hard on a new attack that I knew would help me even a slight degree.

GAVIN: Okay, ready for round 2?

ANUBIS: Hm?

I got up, dusted myself off, and got ready to test out the move as energy started to spark from my hands.

GAVIN: I'll show you the stinger!

I made a quick, sharp pointed edge from my aura and held it in one hand. I wanted it to be as sharp as a harpoon, but unlike a sharp weapon, this is like a mini bomb. It's not as strong as the fox fire, but it's quick and easy to step up. I threw it at Anubis, and just as expected, he dodged it. It got stuck right behind him on the ground as he looked at me even angrier.

ANUBIS: Is that all? I expected more.

GAVIN: *Kaboom.*

I snapped my fingers, and the attack detonated right after, catching Anubis off guard. This was my chance to end this fight with one move. I quickly charged a fox fire and ran into the smoke of where Anubis was to get a direct hit at point-blank. I slid into the smoke, but he vanished. I quickly looked around to see if he had jumped into the air like I did.

GAVIN: Wait, wher—?

ANUBIS: Great try, kit. *My turn.*

Out of nowhere he popped out of the ground and hit me square in the jaw as I stumbled back in pain, then he grabbed me by the face, pulling me up to his eye level.

ANUBIS: I'll give you credit. You're the first in a long time
to even come close to hurt me. But it'll take more than
tricks to beat me.

He fired a blast of sand directly at my chest, launching me onto the
floor again. I had no clue how to even get in close to him, but there had
to be a way. I got up again and got another stinger ready. If I could hit
him with a direct hit, then it would stun him long enough for a dead-on
fox fire. I got up and made another stinger, and Anubis was looking at
me, wondering why I was holding another.

ANUBIS: You think that trick will work twice?

GAVIN: *Wanna bet that?*

I ran toward Anubis, stinger in hand, and started a little sword fight.
With a few swings, I forced Anubis back into a defensive position. For
a second, I thought I was getting somewhere till he sighed.

ANUBIS: Your form is absolutely terrible. You're leaving
yourself wide open to hits. Like here, and here, and
here, and here!

With each "here," he would slam into a different part of my body. I
was getting too tired to fight back, and I did one last move in desperation

GAVIN: And you fight to be noble because you're wide open
here.

I faked a swing as I kicked him right in the crotch to both our
discomforts. It felt like hitting a hard pile of compacted sand as I just
dealt with the pain. The attack did give me enough time to hit directly
for the stinger right in his chest and charge another fox fire.

GAVIN: It's over. *Fox fire!*

I aimed right at his head with a point-blank hit on Anubis. I thought
I had won as the smoke started to clear to just sand in the room. It was
quiet for a bit as I looked around for him again. I think I actually won
the fight.

GAVIN: I did it? *I did it?! I did it!*

ANUBIS: No, you didn't.

I turned around in a panic as I fell to the ground, limping from all attacks. He was back inside his casket, but he was smiling. The weird thing was that he looked like he was turning into sand. I don't think he dodged my attack as well as he thought.

ANUBIS: You could've never beat me, but you are a crafty
    one. I'm sure you'll do fine.

GAVIN: What? W-wait, fine for what?

ANUBIS: This was all a test. You'll do fine out in this world.
    I wonder what your full power will look like?

He pulled out a bright red box from behind him, glancing back over to me.

ANUBIS: I think what you've been searching for is in there.
    Good luck, kit.

He tossed it to me and just disappeared into the wind.

GAVIN: What? Why did he? But huh?

I don't I'll ever get what that meant by that, but he did teach me some basics in sword fighting. But it wasn't till he left did I realize the fact that I just fought Anubis, a god, an actual god.

GAVIN: *Wait a second, does this mean that gods actually exists!?*

CHAPTER

20

I opened the box Anubis gave me, and a red spirit came out. The sand and wind blew around the room, and I closed my eyes again.

GAVIN: Hey there, sorry about the delay.

RED: I'm thankful you finally got me out of there and that you survived too.

GAVIN: So you're the second spirit. You said there were four of you, right? Don't worry, I'll rescue the last two as fast as I can. I already made a promise to Blue about it.

RED: That's comforting news. I'll have to show my thanks to you sometime soon. I should start by leading you free from here first. To get out of here, you're going to have to climb up into that coffin.

I looked over to the coffin as the red spirit started to float around it.

RED: What are you waiting for? Hop on in.

GAVIN: Uh, okay.

I stumbled toward the empty coffin, hopping inside as the coffin sealed tight. It then felt like I was being tossed and tumbled around, with several breaking sounds that could be the only thing I heard, when suddenly, it all stopped. I pushed with all my might, and the coffin popped open. I looked outside to see that I was in a storage unit behind the museum. It was still as quiet as the last time as I hopped out the coffin, stretching a bit. My entire body was screaming out in pain, and I just wanted to go home and sleep. I was about to find an exit when the sound of meowing caught my attention. It was the same cat from before, standing right next to a window.

GAVIN: Okay, that's it. You're just too weird now.

I hopped up the boxes, and the cat just sat and stared at me as I got closer. I bent down to the cat, and I tilted his head angrily at me.

GAVIN: Really, what is your deal? Are you the one following me?

CAT: …

GAVIN: And now I'm talking to a weird cat. Heh, okay then.
But really, you're one weird guy.

The cat nodded, keeping its angry expression as it looked around me a bit, before sitting back down, licking its paws.

GAVIN: Well, I'm going home. Later, a weird cat.

The cat meowed back loudly, and I hopped out the window into the cool, crisp night air.

—⟋⟍—

FULTING: I can't believe you got solid info about the fox. Great work, RH.

LIGHTER: Yeah, great job, RH. Let's just hope they weren't lying.

The three staked out the building and watched for any movements that drew their attention.

LIGHTER: All right, team, the plan is simple. When we see 'em, me and Fulting will use ourselves as a distraction. RH, use your ice to freeze it in place, long enough to place the tracker on it. From there, we start asking questions.

FULTING: So we're not killing it, right?

LIGHTER: Unless it gives us a reason.

RH gave a little sigh as they all heard meowing from an area of the museum. They watched the building like hawks, then the fox came out hopping from the top of the building onto another. Lighter looked at his comrades before getting up from his seated position.

LIGHTER: All right, team. Break.

—⚍—

By the time I finally got out, it was almost three in the morning. I would barely get any sleep tonight for sure, but the thing that was on my mind at the moment was the same feeling from before: That I was being watched again. I thought it was that cat, but the feeling was very distant. I stopped on top of a building to look around a bit, and I tried to see if anyone was around. The only sounds I heard were the sounds of cars or birds close by, but it felt like someone was right behind me. The smell of flowers filled my nose again. I turned around, and I saw the same strange girl from a few days ago. She was staring at me, then sat down, looking at the stars. Was this girl also following me?

GAVIN: Hey, who—

GIRL: So you saved two of them already, and so soon. You should prepare yourself. The next trails ahead of you will be troublesome.

GAVIN: Save them? Wait, you know about spirits too?

The girl stood up and started to walk over to the edge of the building without answering my question. She took one more step over the edge, and I tried to run over to her. She fell off the building, and I could only look over the edge. Nothing. I was standing right where I originally was and just stared into the night sky. I shook my head a bit as I tried to figure out what the hell just happened. I shook away the weird feeling and started to run again, leaping from building to building, trying to slip in a short cut anywhere I could so I could get home.

LIGHTER: *Hey, fox breath!*

GAVIN: Huh? Oh, it's you again. Hey, how ya been?

LIGHTER: Wha—? Why are you?

GAVIN: Look, I would love to chitchat about stuff, but I got
a lot on my plate right now. We can fight some other
time.

I started to run in a different direction when a bolt of thunder
landed right in front of me.

FULTING: Not till you answer some things we want to know.

GAVIN: Oh, you're here too?

And just on cue, the red-hat guy tried to freeze my feet, and I was
surrounded by the three.

GAVIN: And that makes three. So a three on one. *How fun.*
Look, I don't want to hurt any of you guys, and we both
want the same end goal, right? To help people? So let's
all just calm down and—*look over there!*

I quickly made a stinger, throwing it at the ground to give me a
smokescreen, and I started to make a run for it. I heard the shouts from
the fire guy. I started to make a run for it, and I felt a fireball zoom
right past me.

LIGHTER: Okay, *this pest is mine.*

FULTING: What?! Just like that?

LIGHTER: Fulting!

FULTING: Fine. Okay then.

It was a giant chase around buildings and corners as I tried my best
to dodge everything they threw at me. The fire, ice, and lighting was
getting to me, especially after fighting Anubis. I was running on fumes.
Actually, running on fumes was an understatement. My entire body felt
like it was crying out for me to stop and rest. I think the saviors could
read my mind, or I was way too distracted from the pain in my leg, as
an instant shock of lightning stunned me in place. I was knocked into
a water tower by a block of pure ice. Then the three all circled around
me. I wanted to keep running, but at that point, I figured I had better
odds trying to talk them down, at least enough for me to get enough
energy to run again.

GAVIN: *Okay, okay, you got me. Can we just talk this out, please? I haven't done anything wrong, right?*

FULTING: Actually, there's a lot I kinda wanted to know. So what are you?

GAVIN: *A kitsune. Next.*

FULTING: And what the hell is that?

GAVIN: *It's a kind of fox. A demon one. You want another one? I can do this this all night.*

LIGHTER: Why you cocky little—

The masked-wearing savior nudged the Lighter person's shoulder, quickly calming him down and focusing him back into the savior that shocked the life out of me.

FULTING: Uh, not too sure what else to ask. Well, are you evil, like you want to—

GAVIN: *Nope, all I want to do…is help…*

They all looked at each other confused, then I started to pull myself back up, coughing a bit before finally getting in a decent breath since I started this night.

FULTING: See, I told you he's not a bad guy.

LIGHTER: *But he is the most infuriating thing on the planet!*

GAVIN: You're a party too.

LIGHTER: Stay out of this.

GAVIN: That's literally what I've been trying to do, but y'all won't let me.

Lighter's arms set up in a strong blaze aimed right for my head before the ice savior placed a hand on his shoulder, trying to calm him down a bit. He quickly did, and I let out a laugh at the moment—a panicked laugh that hurt like hell as they all looked back at me with way more focus than before.

GAVIN: Okay then. All jokes aside, what do y'all actually want to know?

118

LIGHTER: Fine, I have a real question. When you broke into Relico, what did you take? And why?

GAVIN: Something special to me. It was a gift from my father. It would've been easy in and out, but I met that ice guy. Also, sorry about the whole leaving you dangling, red-hat man.

LIGHTER: RH is a girl, you ignoramus.

GAVIN: What, he's a she? Sorry again. I really don't want any trouble.

RH nodded in approval. At the very least, two of them seemed to kinda like me.

GAVIN: So last one 'cause I really got to go. Just ask.

LIGHTER: What do you know about the shadows? No tricks or jokes.

GAVIN: Oh, those things. Well, from what I was told—

I explained to them everything that I could piece together. About the spirits being locked away, the calamity, and why I'm going after the shards in the first place. I even told them who I just fought and the rather embarrassing method of how I was able to beat them.

FULTING: So let me get this straight. We're all fucked if this *calamity* or whatever gets out?

GAVIN: Apparently, or that's what I got from them. There might also be a chance that it's already out, but I wouldn't know. All I know is that I need those shards to save the other two spirits

FULTING: Fuck.

GAVIN AND LIGHTER: Language.

The two of us looked at each other. For some reason instead of understanding, I felt intimidated by him. I guess he didn't believe me or, worse, still wants me dead.

GAVIN: You know when you guys aren't trying to kill me, you guys are pretty cool.

LIGHTER: You're still annoying.

GAVIN: And you're still an ass.

FULTING: Wait, why are you doing this alone? We could ask the boss to get you on the team! Forget the whole *we're out to beat you stick*, you could join us!

GAVIN: Man, I would love to. Really, I would. B-but with my current rep, I think I'll pass. I'll help you guys out when I can though.

LIGHTER: You're a weird one, aren't yeah?

GAVIN: Heh, yeah. Well then, I think I should get out of all of your hair, right? See ya around.

I left in a hurry and ran as fast as I could. Not home, just out of sight. I wanted to trust them. I really did, but I had this feeling that told me to stick around for a bit.

GAVIN: Okay, what did they actually want?

Blue popped beside me to follow my train of thought as I listened to what they were saying after I left.

LIGHTER: So did you get the tracker on him?

RH nodded as she gave a passive thumbs-up.

LIGHTER: Great, now we find out where the thing goes. That talk with him was interesting, but he could be dangerous if left unchecked.

FULTING: It's really a shame. He seems like a really nice person, right? He might even have a good taste for food.

LIGHTER: Not now with the food, Fulting.

I looked around at my clothing. Trying to see if anything was different about it, I found a small device on one of my shoes. So that's why they wanted to freeze my feet so badly. I wanted to just break it right there and then, but I came up with a better idea. I took the small device and ran to Relico Inc. and left a note for them. I hope they like it because I was in way too much pain from just writing it. After that pit stop, I finally went home and was greeted by my mother waiting for me in the darkness of my room. The level of dream I felt while staring back at her was way more than any shadow ever could try to place on me.

MOM: *Gavin, in all my life, I have never—*

GAVIN: Yep, all well that ends well.

—⚋—

MAX: So where does the tracker lead?

ZACK: It says, back at Relico? Oh no.

The three of them got back and found the tracker next to a note:

> *Hey, y'all drop this! See ya soon!*
> *The Kitsune*

ZACK: That *sneaky, little, cocky mother fu—*

MAX: Language.

ZACK: *Say another word and I'll beat you into the next wall over.*

The two boys continued to argue back and forth as RH left them to fix their own problems. This night had dragged on long enough, and she had more than enough drama for one night. She waved the boys off to Zack, who'd already had Max in a chokehold from his previous comment. She started to make her way down the labyrinth maze of halls to find her room.

Ever since the fox had snuck in, Eugene had been scrambling to make the company's security more secure, which still didn't make sense to her. The thought was about to leave her mind till she noticed Eugene at the end of a hallway seemingly talking with a robed figure. She walked past the hall, swearing that for a moment she saw vines coming from the figure's legs, before getting curious and going back to check on him. The second she did, both people had vanished out of thin air. She was about to take a step toward where they were when a hand touched her shoulder.

EUGENE: Welcome back. I saw that you and your team left in a hurry. I hope that it was worth it, going without notifying me about your plans.

RH quickly jumped away from her boss to be met with his tired and apathetic frown. He let out a heavy sigh as she started to walk past the frightened warrior.

EUGENE: Either case, get some rest. I still need to run more tests on you three. Or rather, you. Something about you in particular is rather *peculiar*, to say the least. Get some rest now.

RH started to relax herself and then tried to leave back to her own room. That was, till Eugene stopped to say one last thing to her.

EUGENE: And before I forget. For your own and those two's sake, *don't go behind my back again. I have enough to deal with. Don't make me add you three to the list.*

RH gave a half-hearted nod to him, then she left the corridor in a hurry and proceeded to lock herself in her room. The slight threat from Eugene was more than enough to make her wish the night never happened as she fell hard into the side of her bed.

EPILOGUE

Molly and the Luna

It's been a few days since I fought Anubis and the saviors. If I'm being honest, the days since then have kinda blurred together. Nothing has happened since then, and I've just been existing in the moment. It was just another day riding the train back home. I was zoning in and out from all the boring school work from today, trying my best to stay awake as Molly bumped my shoulder in anger trying to sew her ribbon. We were on a train home, but I wasn't paying attention to anything other than getting home and passing out in my bed.

MOLLY: God, I can't focus on this. Where do these loops even go?

GAVIN: *Would work a lot better if you weren't rushing it.*

MOLLY: What was that?

GAVIN: *Nothing. Just take your time. It looks like you're almost done.*

MOLLY: Not really, I still have—

The train then suddenly froze as the lights went out. An intercom came over saying that a small outage caused the trains to be out of commission for a bit. We were the only ones in the train at the time as I didn't take much problem with it. I looked over to Molly as she had already dropped the sewing materials for her ribbon, looking out the window. It was a beautiful sight really. The setting sun on the sea, being illuminated more by the city lights. I just didn't care cause I just felt so tired. I started to nod off, then I felt something tap my shoulder. Thinking that it was Molly, I tried to brush it off.

GAVIN: *Molly, please leave me alone, I'm kinda tired right now.*

MOLLY: Oh really? You're tired... *I wish I could say the same.*

GAVIN: Huh?

I opened my eyes back up, and she was still staring outside. I finally got a look at her. She was silently crying. I snapped out of my tiredness. I was confused. I should've been better attentive of her.

GAVIN: Molly, are you okay? What's wrong? I'm sorry, I'm up.

MOLLY: I'm sorry it's just been kinda rough. My grandparents keep telling me that *I need to focus up on my future* and other shit. They keep saying that I should have a plan that isn't *outdoor filth*. I'm sick of hearing it. I just want to do what I want to do. I like exploring. I like the feeling of mud, dirt, sand—all of it. I want to get out of this place. I hate this doctor stuff they want me to learn, and for what? The second I can, I'm leaving this place. I'm gonna take my bags, flip my grandparents off, and just leave.

GAVIN: Uh woah, that's uh.

MOLLY: Yeah, I know. Ugh, why is life so unfair? I wish I was that fox and stuff. If I were them, I'd run far away. Be as free as a bird.

GAVIN: T-the fox? Heh, heh, yeah. I guess so.

MOLLY: You guess so?

GAVIN: Well, I'm just saying, what if they're sticking around for a reason? Like a p-protector and stuff. Isn't that a reason?

Molly looked at me, wiping off her tears, before returning to her more hyper attitude.

Molly: Gavin, if you're scared about me leaving, we'll stay in touch and stuff. You're my best friend. Hell, maybe I should take you with me. With your book smarts and my raw power, we could do everything!

Gavin: *Except find you a girlfriend—*

She instantly started to blush as she smacked me lightly in the face. I decided to lightly fight back as the two of us started to run around the train car having a blast before we both settled down looking out the window again.

Molly: Hey, you're finally starting to fight back, I see.

Gavin: I guess you could say I grew a backbone. Are you feeling any better?

Molly: Yeah, a lot better. Thanks, man.

We both just looked out the window, continuing to enjoy the view, before she looked at me again.

Molly: You seem so perfect, with your good grades and stuff. What's your deep, dark secret? Let me guess. You plan on going to regular college and not nerd college.

Gavin: Ha-ha, but for your information, I don't have secrets. I'll tell you that right out the gate.

Molly: Oh really? Then did you ever once have a crush on me?

Gavin: No, next question.

Molly: Wha—never took you as a liar.

Gavin: It's the truth, we're friends and nothing more.

Molly: Oh, really. So if I were to *die tragically*, then you'd just be normal sad and not sad, sad?

Gavin: Of course not, I'd never let you die in the first place. I'll promise you that.

Molly: Okay then. Hey, look over there! Seagulls!

GAVIN: You mean rats with wi—

The train lights spurted back to life, and Molly looked back at me with a smile.

GAVIN: Oh, that does remind me, you said you did have an eye on someone, right? Maybe the three of us can hang out as a group or something.

Her face instantly turned red as her shoulders started to droop down into themselves.

MOLLY: Well, *change of subject*. Tests are coming up. I have a feeling that I'll do okay. You?

GAVIN: Eh, good enough. It'll be easy as usual.

We shared a laugh for a bit till she stopped looking, slightly concerned.

MOLLY: Hey, you don't look good. You okay? I've been meaning to ask you this, but why does it always look like you have a scar on your neck?

GAVIN: I don't have a scar on my neck?

MOLLY: *All right then.*

She sat back down as the train moved around again. I guess I didn't say the right thing again. I didn't mind as I just closed my eyes and sighed. It felt strangely nice to just relax like this. I'll just wait till Molly gets off to fully take a nap.

—◊—

As the young man's mind started to fade out into a slight rest, his friend had other things on her mind.

MOLLY: *I know he's lying about something, I'm not sure what, but he is. I just have this feeling that he's putting way too much on him. It's just that smile he puts on, like it hurts to hold. I was lying about the scar, but as I watched over him while in the train cart, I swear that for a split second, I saw this almost black gel of some kind float around the room before disappearing. Gavin, what's wrong with you?*

126

www.ingramcontent.com/pod-product-compliance
Lightning Source LLC
Chambersburg PA
CBHW050825180626
46814CB00004B/1462